Depths & Dragons

HUGH FOX

I0554420

SKYLIGHT
PRESS

First published in Great Britain by Skylight Press,
210 Brooklyn Road, Cheltenham, Glos GL51 8EA

Designed and typeset by Rebsie Fairholm
Cover photographs by Rebsie Fairholm
Printed and bound in Great Britain

www.skylightpress.co.uk

ISBN 978-1-908011-07-7

For Menke Katz,
who brought me to the top of the right mountain
at the right (perfect) moment.

I

"I'm so hungry!" Adam kept insisting, insisting, insisting.

Miriam wanting to tell him "Shut up, *tum'tum*/idiot!" give him a good crack, tell him to play with his damned Game Cube and leave her alone. Tel Aviv in the middle of summer. Theoretically a sensual, luxurious, beach-filled heaven-on-earth, but their air-conditioner just didn't make it. Top floor. The roof like a pizza pan in the middle of an oven.

And all the craziness, never ever, for one moment, day or night, feeling really relaxed-relaxed, always expecting something-something-something to happen.

Why didn't Adonai-Elohainu just reappear and set things straight the way He used to do in the past… past… passover… pass over into a new epoch of peace, instead of allowing all this artificial enmity to go on and on, herself almost looking like an Arab, or she could have passed for a Hindu, couldn't she, hand me my sari and let me start a new life with a red dot on my forehead.

Getting up, kissing Adam on the head.

"Just relax, pal, your dad will be back in just a few moments with some delicious pizza…"

The table already set.

Some nice (imported) peach juice. Imported from Georgia, no less. Not Georgia-Russia, but USA Georgia.

Michael happily in front of the TV watching some crazy French film called *Mondo*. DVD. Spoken French, French subtitles. Studying French in school … and it had kind of taken over, hadn't it … French, French, French, French.

She wanted him to be an M.D. *He'd* wanted, had said he wanted, to become an M.D., and now all this French.

"They always need French teachers. France isn't going to go away," he'd laughed at her the other day when she'd quietly complained about such a complete immersion in French culture.

At least he was calm, not like Mr Fussy, Adam…

Standing looking out the window at the beach.

So many people. Miami-ish.

And she couldn't blame Michael, could she, she was the big Francophile around here, every night a little French film, as much as Mr Big Biz-Banker Mort could take, *Camille Claudel, Jean de Florette, Le Chat, Manon des Sources* … loving her new DVD's capability (a Passover gift from Mort) of putting the subtitles in French, while you listened to the French itself, one continuous "class" in French, better than the lit classes she'd been taking over at the University of Tel Aviv, although she loved them too … her biggest problem a little Madame Bovaryish, just 'bored,' wanting to get a job as an artist, even if it was commercial art, or wanting to get her paintings into an exhibition, make it big as an artist, post-impressionist, but nothing kinky-crazy-forced modern, just *la réalité, la réalité, la réalité…*

Mort always telling her, "Just wait until the boys are a little older and more on their own. They need 'mothering.' What could be more important than that?"

"Nothing!" she always had to admit, in fact sometimes afraid of what would happen when they *were* grown, gone, away, and she was this frail little old lady making her way into the synagogue on Friday nights with Mort half holding her up, "Shabbat Shalom, Shabbat Shalom…" part of an ever-aging village of oldsters … but like Rabbi Greiman always told her when she voiced her fears about aging, "The other alternative, death, isn't too attractive either, is it? It comes soon enough, believe me…"

Both their parents already dead, her father killed by shrapnel from a bomb when he was out walking his poodle, her mother dying six months later from a long, endlessly long cancer, both of Mort's parents dead from heart problems, and Mort already with one carotid-artery-cleaning-out job to his credit … the words from the Kaddish too often flowing through her head, *Yit-ga-dal ve-yit-ka-dash* / Let the glory of God be extolled, let His great name be hallowed … not really 'remembering' the dead at all, but merely praising God, the God of Life the God of Death, spreading his mantle across the whole universe…

"Mummy, I'm hungry too … really hungry!"

Michael this time. Mr Nerd.

"This is getting serious!" she laughed, went into the fridge and got out some cokes.

"OK, you guys … he'll be back in a moment, *daka, daka, daka…*"

Handing them the cokes, taking one for herself, opening a bag of crisps, barbecue-flavoured, thinking of ham for a moment, the time in New York when she had some barbecue spare-ribs and ate them before she realised they were pork, pork, pork…

Not that she believed that much in the kosher-laws, but still shrimp and pork were off her list, although she loved the taste of pork more than anything else in the world except turrons in southern France, pistachios and candied orange and cherries, vanilla and nuts.

Standing at the window again, feeling suddenly sleepy. Oh, to just stretch out on her bed and waft away into nothingness, dissolve into dreamlessness, that was her idea of heaven, out, out, out…

When suddenly there was this huge explosion somewhere not far away.

God! Not a moment of peace!

And she'd almost escaped from her constant gnawing fear for a moment. Almost escaped.

How about just going someplace where The Madness hadn't reached yet? Like the Pyrenees … northern Spain, southern France. Couldn't he run his financial business via computers the way he did right now?

Michael and Adam both running over to her, hanging on to her legs, around her waist.

"What's that, Mum?"

"Probably something horrible!"

Smelling the smoke now, gunpowder stench. *Oh-seh shalom bimromav, hu ya'aseh shalom* … May He who causes peace to reign in the high heavens, let peace descend on us…

Not knowing what to do.

Suddenly afraid for Mort, out there on the battlefield of the streets, wanting to go out, run down the stairs, go out into the streets herself.

"What about Daddy?" Michael suddenly prescient, prophetic, not young boyish any more but grandfatherly …

either that or one year old again, everything in hand, richness, fullness, completion, and then suddenly the madness of nothing, nothing at all. *klum, meu'ma, shum davar'*…

"I'll go out, see what's going on," disentangling herself from the both of them, like two octopi, "come on, you guys…" finally free, "you stay here now, no matter what…" then wondering if that was good advice or not, shouldn't they all just flee, run away, escape, who knew what was coming next, sometimes these things came chained together, in clusters. But… opening the door. One last contradictory order. "If anything else happens…" Stopping. What do you do on the last apocalyptic day of the world? "Just stay here, period!"

Out into the streets. Sirens all over the place. People running from what was obviously the centre of the explosion.

Being stopped by a trooper in camouflage battle-garb.

"This area is cordoned off. No one allowed in…"

"My husband…"

A young Jewish guy, very nerdy looking under his helmet, she bet that off-duty he was some kind of total computer nerd, she could just see him, Sony, Sony, Sony, CDs, DVDs… computer games…

Hesitating. His face filled with confusion, decision-making.

"Well…" smiling, "I didn't see you… but be careful… you never know…"

"OK."

Down the narrow street into the heart of confusion and smoke and noise, down to the pizza parlour where Mort had gone, half a block gone, just where the pizza parlour had been, wanting to just stop, just die, thinking about death so much these days anyhow, her death, the death of Israel, the holocaust, this whole madness like the holocaust reborn, continued … never seeing life so short, looking at her boys sometimes and imagining them old men, like it happened in a day, the universe so endless and timeless, and this tiny earth just a dot in the midst of all the stars and who knows what else, sometimes at night walking along the beach and looking up on a clear night and with all the millions and millions of stars looking down on her, feeling like nothing, nothing at all…

Soldiers, Red Cross workers, stretchers, carrying out bodies.

Stopping. Just stopping and starting to cry as she watched the bodies being carried by her, all maimed, half there, blood all over them, half a face, both legs gone, blood still dribbling out of a stomach wound.

"You really shouldn't be here!"

A colonel this time.

"My husband."

"I'll repeat myself. You really shouldn't be here …"

Not pushing her, twisting her, turning her, but almost.

"I …"

Turning, just as she saw … no, it couldn't be … the top of his head all blown off, the whole right side, his face full of blood, being carried on a stretcher right by her. No, it couldn't be, God wouldn't allow it, looking up at the blinding, bright sky … no, it couldn't be …

"It's my …"

Rushing over to him, out of control now, embracing the body, making the stretcher-carriers stop.

The colonel not quite sure what to do, but falling back on rules and regulations.

"Really, I'll have to ask you to…"

Letting his body go, her arms full of blood too now, this sudden horrible realisation that he was gone, gone forever, there was no reason to be there at all, Mort, his Mort-ness, essence, whatever he really was, gone…

Standing watching them carry him away, the colonel approaching her, "Maybe I should get an identification from…"

Walking away from him, following the stretcher-bearers for a moment, but when they put the body in an ambulance at the corner, just walking on as if she were in some kind of trance, drunk, crazy, under the influence of some sort of shaman-producing drug, a zombie, ghost, not in the real world any more, not thinking, some slight little voices inside her telling her not to go home, not this way, covered with blood, or to go to a police station somewhere and tell them her husband had been killed, or … or … or …

Instead just walked back home, blood on the lift buttons as she pushed them, bloody tracks as she walked down the hall to her apartment. But she didn't care if she got blood all over the carpet, didn't care if there were any carpet at all, any apartment, her fancy rattan and wicker furniture that she'd made such a point of getting because it was so 'beachy,' so 'light,' so 'up,' 'vacationy,' as if Tel Aviv were some sort of Middle Eastern Miami Beach instead of what it *really* was, a cauldron of death, a zombie playing-field, murder-centre, for thousands and thousands of years, and it never would end, would it, but would remain a kind of slaughter-ground forever and forever, Amen.

Her two boys in the kitchen eating kosher hotdogs at the kitchen table.

So they couldn't wait, huh.

Grabbing the hotdogs out of their hands and throwing them out the front window.

"My God, what's wrong? What happened?" screamed Michael. "Are you crazy? You have to go to the hospital … I can call an ambulance…"

Taking their little mobile phone off the coffee table in the living room, their favourite phone, as if a phone attached to a wall was the enemy now, it had to be one hundred percent portable, up-to-date, grabbing it out of his hand and throwing it out the window too, "You won't be needing this any more!" scaring the hell out of him … and Adam. Both of them backing away down the hall toward the lockable bathroom, Michael screaming at her, "Dad is dead, isn't he?"

How could he have known?

How could he have not known?

Going into the living room and standing in front of the rattan sofa with its dark green cushions, one of her prizes furniturewise…

"Fuck it!"

Letting herself fall down on it, arms outstretched, head back, wailing, wailing, wailing like a wild animal, then her face into her hands, crying, would there ever be a time when she could stop…?

Michael coming over to her and trying to comfort her.

"So what happened?"

"Your father's dead, that's what happened…"

"So what are we going to do?"

"Do? It's done…"

Suddenly up on her feet, running over toward the balcony, out to the railing, thirteen stories down, thirteen a lucky number for Jews, so they said, looking down, down, down … down at the street below, the concrete, the cars, wanting to just jump, end it all, what was the point, not believing in any afterlife, really, no matter what anyone (always vaguely) said, remembering some prayer somewhere in the liturgy about "resting in the dust," that's what she wanted, to rest in the dust, for all eternity, rest in the dust, dust, dust…

Then Adam, the blesséd clown, coming up behind her with a beach bucket filled with water and a dishcloth from the kitchen, kneeling down and starting to wash her legs.

Crazy angel.

Alive again, no past, no future, nothing but her little monkey-ape on his knees washing her bloody legs, while Michael held on to her, not so much to keep her from jumping but holding on to her like she were some sort of all-supporting tree, God Himself come down to comfort him, like he was two again and he'd just fallen down in the playground, holding on, holding on, starting to cry, as Adam-Monkey kept washing her legs, moved up to the arms, then went into the house, came back with a new, clean dress for her, and wordlessly handed it to her, not like he was her son at all, but her long, long, long dead mother.

II

She loved Paris, period. Wasn't much that she didn't love.

Loved to simply walk along the Seine, practically anywhere, the trees, the lovers, *l'histoire*, especially now that she'd been (rather painfully) immersing herself in French history, literature, re-enforcing what she already knew about Satie and Baudelaire, Monet, Renoir, Apollinaire ... dragging herself through the Louvre over and over again during the afternoons before she picked up *les enfants* at school, Adam more confused than she was at their sudden immersion in French culture after ten years of pure Hebrew-Israeli-Jewish everything, although in a way Michael was already at home, given his long-term penchant for everything *française*.

"How long are we going to stay here?" Adam had asked the night before as she bent down to kiss him as he lay there in his bed, sleepy as a drunken dormouse, "I miss the beach..."

"France has beaches too. Not too far ... if we can just save a little money. If I could write a book about my leaving Israel and coming to Paris..."

"If you could find a new husband ... there has to be someone over at Am Echod..."

Which gave her the giggles. And made her feel ashamed.

Not that she'd forgotten Mort, engulfed as he was in tragedy, never able to undo that final image on the stretcher, half his head gone, all drenched in his own blood, like some sort of (non-Kosher style) slaughtered ox.

But it was true, it seemed a trifle remote now ... all of it ... the whole ancient war of Israel for its own territory, Babylonians, Philistines, Egyptians, Palestinians ... whoever, whoever, whoever, especially when...

La pluie est fraîche,
le vent est bon.
The rain is fresh,
the wind is good.

Loved Artaud. Struggled through him with her Hebrew-French dictionary.

It was so nice to be able to speak Hebrew with Rabbi

Frankel over at Am Echod, even if it was work, work, work, major work for him. Good for him.

Sometimes in unguarded, off moments an image coming into her mind of them together, completely naked, in the midst of high passion.

Shame, shame…

Although how could he stand that groundhog wife of his with her intolerable hats and shoes and bowed-legs and gold glasses and vanity, vanity, vanity?

And there was always a touch of, what would you call it, 'flirtation,' in the air:

Il dit non avec la tête
mais il dit oui avec le coeur…
He says no with his head
but he says yes with his heart…
Forget it, forget it!

Walking down the left bank toward Notre Dame now, thinking of Hemingway and Fitzgerald and Henry Miller … the avant-garde American literary gang here in the twenties, before World War II …

Too much reading, she was becoming such a nerd.

But loving the trees along the Seine, especially now that autumn was arriving, the summer heat was gone, it was almost chill, and most of the tourists had left.

Why so attracted to Notre Dame?

It was as if her subconscious had taken over her legs and she was walking there not *against* her will, but without any will at all, dreamlike, *dans un rêve*.

Thinking all sorts of … what would you call them, 'sacrilegious' thoughts?

Judaism didn't give any ultimate answers, did it, God up there in the sky somewhere, pulling up and pulling down the sun and moon, keeping the stars in place, blessing us with life … and death.

Kaddish again, *per omnia saecula saeculorum*, for all time-eternity, *haolam*. She should have never bought the missal she'd bought two weeks ago … the prayers for the dead full of Hollywoodish heavens, clouds and angels and … that other book she'd got on Catholicism … the Beatific Vision, pushed

13

to the peak of all possible pleasure, forever and forever, Amen.

Not like Kaddish, where all you did was praise God, praise God, praise God.

A street vendor up ahead. Wraps. A little chicken wrap wouldn't hurt her.

Everything from the street-vendors in Paris always so good.

"Treat yourself a little," her voices inside her whispering. She was doing OK teaching at the Am Echod Hebrew school, although sometimes she thought that Rabbi Frankel was overpaying her, something under-the-table-ish about it all, because she was a survivor from Israel, a widow whose husband had been practically pulverized by The Enemy, because she was *her…*

A big mirror in the window of an antique store, something very Italianate, nineteenth centuryish, nicely carved wooden scrolls, obviously the mirror itself new, stopped and looked at herself in it…

The darkish perfect skin, very black eyes and black (dyed) hair, the little hat-cap, ankles and legs so amazingly slim, remembering her buba even when she was in her forties, how her ankles had swollen up and stayed that way, probably the tight stockings she always wore, tight bands around the tops cutting off circulation, like pouring yourself into liquid nylon pantyhose.

Rabbi Frankel back again, looking at her, as if he were embarrassed somewhere deep inside himself, embarrassed for being, for … *being in love with her*?

Not that she could blame him, thinking about his wife again, Sarah's, stubby little fatsy-watsy legs. Not to mention her face, always looking like she'd just eaten a hot pepper.

And how did she feel about him?

'Horny' wasn't the word. Not 'physical', really but missing another body against hers, missing naked contact, penetration, climaxing, then the collapse back on the bed, someone in her arms and her in someone's arms, like two naked babies sleeping together, beyond sex altogether … thinking about 'heaven' again … what did they call it, extreme unction? No that was something else…

Going over to the street vendor, who looked very 'arabish,' not Palestinian but further northern, maybe into Jordan or Afghanistan. Tempted to try a little Arabic on him, *mais non, non, non…*

"A chicken wrap, *s'il vous plaît…*"

Smiling, very gracious.

Très cher, but so what, everything in Paris was expensive, especially around here, 'downtown.' Thrifty always thrifty in spite of being 'loaded' (in the bank/stocks/investments, like 'theory') happy to have found such a nice (albeit tiny) place in a working class neighbourhood. One bedroom, so let the kids sleep in it, she didn't mind the sleeper-sofa, and the traffic noise outside that she'd thought would have bothered her, actually seemed to soothe her to sleep … although she missed the sound of the sea that she'd loved so much in Tel Aviv. Feeling sometimes guilty about just how much she had in the bank, the interest that she (mainly) lived on, even letting a little bit flow back into the capital itself.

Sea, sea, sea … why such a fascination with the sea?

In the beginning … the sea in the beginning … as if we were all just sea-things that had made their way by chance to land.

Thinking about the Gospel of, what was it, John: *In the beginning was the Word, and the Word was God, and the Word was with God* … Why was she reading the gospels at all? Almost as if it were a 'sin.' Was she picking up the Catholic-Christian sense of 'sin' too? Christ was the 'Word' spoken by God the Father. Only if the Messiah was Jesus of Nazareth, why wasn't the world inflated with, what could you call it, 'messiah-ness?' saved, jubilant, rejoicing, instead of *toujours, toujours triste*/forever, forever sad? If there were *any* God up there why didn't He step out on a cloud or something and bang His sceptre on the earth and stamp out violence, appear in all His glory and stop the crap?

Melech Haolam! / King of the Universe! Why would any king allow his universe to degenerate into such a mess?

Bit into the wrap. Ahhhhhhh … better than sex. Blue cheeseish, roquefortish, with a touch of humus, which made the vendor an Arab, *n'est ce pas*?

Reminding her of the kibe sandwiches/wraps her mother used to buy her on the streets of Tel Aviv and Jerusalem when she was a kid, before all this crap had begun.

Finding a bench next to the river and sitting down.

Something to drink?

No … don't spoil it with anything else … chew it slowly, savour it, and then later a coke … a beer …

Paris so romantic … all the fancy stores and apartment buildings, the river itself so carefully tended and contained in stone channels … so romantic, if you didn't think about kings and revolutions and guillotines and riots and World War II and Buchenwald…

Shushing herself.

"Quiet! Quiet! Calm!"

Reading Suzuki's *Zen Mind, Beginner's Mind* right now, kind of Talmudish-Kabbalistic, calm, calm, calm, let the negative flow through you to the Great Sea of Nothingness … as if all we were was flowers, a brief blooming and then *shalom*, peace, peace, peace…

Enjoying the leaves on the maple tree over her, enjoying the bright white, clouded-over sky, almost crisp already, early September, the High Holidays coming up, which she'd have to go to, wouldn't she, being part of the faculty at the Am Echod Hebrew School and all, but which she had begun to hate, the endlessness of it all, all the self-recrimination, asking God for forgiveness…

For what?

She felt almost saintly, sinless … alone, sexless, chaste, pure, a good mother, a good teacher, a good friend…

Lo, lo, lo, lo … Thou Shalt Not!

Shalt not what?

Adultery, theft, murder.

Maybe Commandment number one: I AM THE LORD THY GOD, THOU SHALT NOT HAVE STRANGE GODS BEFORE THEE.

Right out of the Douay version of the bible that she'd bought.

Wasn't Jesus a 'strange' god.

Echod, echod, echod. One … no trinities … but sometimes, when she was walking along she could almost *feel* the Holy

Spirit/Espiritu Santo fluttering around her shoulders like a chiffon ghost … Heilige Geist … where had she read about the Anglo-Saxon (or was it German?) Heilige Geist, Holy Ghost … which they'd modified to Holy Spirit.

No ghosts, just spirits.

OK, *warm me , Holy Spirit, cuddle around my shoulders like a warm, wool shawl.* Making a big effort to get out of her head any speculations and simply enjoy the sandwich that she carefully held so it wouldn't drip on her brown knit blouse, not looking forward to the real cold, having to get her coats out of the wardrobe, coats and boots … and worry about the boys getting cold … which they always did, no matter what she did.

Missing the heat of Tel Aviv, the whole Israeli coast.

Loving Lebanon. Past tense now … loving the sound of Arabic next to Hebrew. Past tense. Loving the intensity of the Arabs themselves. Past tense. Arab food … no, that didn't have to be past tense.

Finishing up the wrap, down to its last fragment of tomato, the last drop of its spicy, minaret-ish juice…

Loving the Alhambra in Sevilla, the way the Jews practically 'ran' Arab Spain. Remembered her Kabbalistic grandfather telling her how he had lived in Safed, the home of the Kabbalah, for years … and loved his Arab neighbours. If the Israelis had just never started 'colonizing' into the middle of what was de facto 'Arab territory' … maybe no conflicts would ever have arisen.

Licking her fingers, taking a handkerchief out of her brown leather purse and wiping her fingers with it. Mrs (Professor) Perfect. The vendor still standing not far away, doing a good business. Waving at him, a little Arabic, "Salaam!" Shalom … and he waved smiling, "Salaam!"

Down to the bridge over to Cité and Notre Dame.

Time for a little art meditation, history-of-cathedrals meditation.

Be honest with yourself, call it what it is, a love-affair with Jesus.

The voices inside her almost (but still not quite!) real voices.

When she'd told the Rabbi about the 'voices' inside her talking, usually contradicting what she was saying, trying to think, he told it was "normal, normal, normal … we all self-dialogue with ourselves … there are all kinds of different fragmented selves inside us, each of them trying to take over."

But she'd gone to a psychiatrist who had wanted to put her on pills.

"We don't psychoanalyse much any more. It's all biochemical now. Pills do it all."

Which she didn't want to get involved with. Took some St. John's Wort for a while, but that seemed to make her worse, was getting just as distrustful of herbs as prescription drugs.

Like the time she'd taken Kava Kava to help her sleep and had turned into a sexed-up madwoman and had actually 'done it' to herself, which she'd never done before.

Two days of Kava Kava, practically climbing roofs. The fiddler on the roof all right … David and Bathsheba … Salome dropping her last veil…

Approaching the front of Notre Dame now, the magnificent facade that invariably inspired awe in her.

"I'm back!" she said to the facade, the towers.

The Virgin Mary with the infant Jesus on her lap, the bible open in his hand, making him a child-scholar, and the Virgin Mary herself carrying a sceptre in her hand, crowned with a beautiful crown, the Queen and her child, no king around except the infant Christ, King of the Universe … *Melech haolam … haolam … olam …* the universe and eternity…

Taking a notebook out of her purse and starting to draw.

The beatifically calm face of the Virgin. Buddhistic. The Buddha of Kamakura, beyond flesh, in a state of absolute calm, what a strange word to come into her head, 'redemptive' … redemptive calm … not that she knew anything about 'redemption.' Except during the high holidays … the rest of the year you were what you were what you were.

The child Jesus.

God becoming man … but really *becoming* man, finding out what *becoming* a man was really about.

Again perfect buddhistic calm.

His right hand up blessing the world.

Was just beginning to sketch in the 'frame' surrounding the virgin and child, the Corinthian columns and then the 'city' on an arch over their head, the City of God speaking to the City of Man...

When a tall, thin priest came walking along.

Old, old, old.

Wondering, do priests *ever, ever* retire? Or was it like the pope – *'til death us do part!*

"*Très joli!* / Very beautiful!"

"*Merci!* / Thanks!"

"Do I detect a bit of a foreign accent in that '*merci*'? *You're from...?* "

"Israel. Tel Aviv."

"Don't tell me. You know about Jews for Jesus?"

"Not really. I'm ... how should I put it... 'my own person.' Not much of a joiner. More rebel than anything else. I do a lot of reading. I've been doing a lot more the last few months. The New Testament. St. Paul, all kinds of books about Catholicism. It seems the second hand bookstores are filled with them. My apartment is starting to turn into a mini-library..."

"Well ... I don't 'pressure' people, but if you're ever interested in, how shall I put it, 'converting,' it's a word that sounds so abrasive, like sandpaper, if you're ever interested in 'sandpapering' your soul..." laughing now, ancient gold glasses that looked like they came out of some flea market somewhere, antique, long hair falling over his forehead, what was he, ninety or something, but very engaging, nothing fake about him, coming on as someone genuine, nothing in it for him, and beside the joviality a deep buddhistic, yes, that was the word, *buddhistic* calm... "my name is Father Peguy ... and, yes, I'm a distant cousin of the writer, do you know Peguy?"

"Not really, I've only been here a little more than a year."

"*Mais vous-parlez très bien ... il semble que vous êtes ici plus que vente années.* / But you speak very well. It seems that you are here more than twenty years."

Inventing, of course. Twenty. Why not make it forty? Why not have me being born in the Bois du Boulogne on the coldest day in Parisian history, turn me into a legend?

"Anyhow, I live here at Notre Dame. In fact I even have a card," going into his trouser pocket, under his black gown, pulling out a card and handing it to her, "I even have an e-mail

… Jesus, the computer nerd," laughing again, then repentant, "I take that back … no joking about redeemers, *n'est ce pas?*"

"*C'est vrai, oui* … that would be like a Rabbi joking about Moses and the ten commandments."

Getting very solemn for a moment.

"We're kind of all the same eggs in the same basket anyhow."

"Only different kinds of birds," she couldn't help but laughing, her old grandmother's genes in her, refusing to take anything, anything, anything serious, even on her deathbed, her last words, "So long, so long, just watch out for those *latkes…*"

Latkes, potato pancakes.

Chanukah.

Wondering, for a quick lightning bolt of a moment, what the connection was between the winter solstice, Christmas (Christ as reborn sun-god?) and Chanukah … and potato pancakes.

"Well, listen … remember … Father Peguy … if you have any questions, anything at all, you know where I am. E-mail, whatever, I love e-mail, don't you? I used to know a Cecilia Guilarte in Toloso, Spain. She'd written a book on Santa Teresa and had written to me because she'd come across my name in her researches, and then I lost contact with her, looked her up on the internet the other day, not expecting to find her, but there she was, dead, unfortunately, but very much alive on the internet…"

"I don't have a computer myself, but there is one over at the synagogue that I use."

"Synagogue?"

"Enghein."

"Oh, yes, I've been there. I love Enghein, Le Lac des Cygnes, even if it is connected to the casino. I'm very, how, shall I put it, transcultural…" taking her hand, smiling, a quick shake, "*Shalom, shalom, shalom* … or as we put it, at least *used* to put it before Vatican II, *Pax Vobiscum…*" let her hand loose and was about to go, but had to put in a few last words, amusing her, seeing him as Father, P.S., P.S., P.S. "I liked Latin, the connection with Rome … the time of Christ's crucifixion … just that little linguistic link to the past."

"What about French?" she laughed, "It's Latin too."

"Not any more," he laughed, and was out the door with a wave, as she continued to draw the Virgin and Christ child, thinking, oddly enough, surprised at how insanely her mind worked, making connections with Jew-boy Christ and the whole Christocentric world that had emerged out of her ancient, ancient Jewish world. Fun, but perhaps a little *dangereux* … for the unity of her sanity/stability. *Nous verrons* … we shall see.

III

Miriam rang the sacristy doorbell gingerly, tentatively, almost fearfully, an old nun in a habit that looked ridiculously out of date opening the door.

"Yes?"

"I'm here to see Father Peguy."

"*Apropos de...?* About...?"

"Conversion."

Suddenly brightening up. Her scowlish look suddenly turning into sunrise.

"Come in, come in..."

Ushering her into a very serious looking room with a crucifix on the wall, the walls lined with books ... thinking Talmud ... although it wasn't Talmud ... bibles ... sets of books ... St. Augustine, St. Ignatius de Loyola...

Feeling like a traitor, really. All the centuries of anti-Jewishness inside the church...

But not really now. A kind of acknowledgement of Jewish 'firstness,' the first ones to come up with such a complete picture of a creator God, although she kept being 'haunted' by the Babylonian and Assyrian pre-Jewish writings, like Hammurabi's *Code* ... in a way it *was* all there, years and years and years before Moses and Genesis.

Confused, tempted for a moment to just get up and leave, just scurry out like an old red hen, no explanations, just out the door into non-confrontational anonymity again ...

Just as Father Peguy came smiling in.

"So it's you. I thought it might be the bishop with news about French priests sexually molesting children." Laughing. But she didn't laugh. "It's so crazy, all that business in the US You know what I think caused it all?"

"What?"

Curious now. Always curious about 'theological' discussions, anything to do with psychology, human behaviour, especially the dastardly and negative.

"Getting rid of Latin, for example. Getting rid of Limbo. Getting rid of nuns' habits ... some sort of mad liberalism that totally de-emphasised the divine nature of revelation."

She'd got up from her tiny little uncomfortable chair when he'd come in. Now Peguy, totally charming, the soul of graciousness and welcoming, told her "Sit down, and none of that hard little chair stuff, try one of the plush ones, so we can talk comfortably."

A row of little stiff chairs, but two big plush leather ones that looked a little *too* plush for church budgets.

"I thought I'd come to see you because … I've been drawing all the sculptures on Notre Dame, Sacré Coeur and other churches. I even went to Chartres and intend to …" getting embarrassed, as always sounding braggy – a braggy Jew, which also amused her, being a stereotype that she could step out of herself and look at.

And he amazingly filled in the blank.

"You intend not to miss a cathedral in France. And then move on to Spain, how about Germany, the Czech Republic. I can just see you making a career out of it – the Cathedrals of Europe. I wouldn't mind joining you. Although, as you might imagine I don't get around much any more. Eighty-three going on what feels like ninety-three…" smiling, a little chuckle, the soul of benevolence and understanding … compassion … that was the word that came into her head … compassion.

"I've got very interested in Catholicism. Lots of reading. I've kind of been haunting used book stores. I love old books, have one whole wall of my little apartment on the Île San Luis filled with books …"

"Which makes a nice decorative touch, *n'est ce pas*? The older the better …"

"The only trouble is that I also read them, and the idea of Jesus being the messiah we've been always waiting for appeals to me, especially making him the son of the Blessed Virgin, although the sexlessness of it all seems kind of …"

"Puritanical?"

"Purit…?"

"Let's call it dualistic, the flesh is evil, the spirit good. *In the Beginning was the Word and the Word was with God* … it had to be a Word that was with God, not – pardon the word – a sperm."

Laughing, looking even more frail and ancient as he laughed, afraid he was going to fall off his chair or something, admiring him for still working, 'carrying on,' which ultimately was better anyhow, wasn't it, instead of just giving in to Death, just waiting for the Angel of Death to appear and tap you on the head with its annihilating wand ...

"But the Catholics praise marriage so highly – the flesh, in marriage anyhow, isn't evil, but good ..."

"The trinity is an interesting – I was going to say 'invention,' but I better watch myself, the Inquisition might have a microphone planted in a bookcase or something," another wide, benevolent, paternal smile.

She loved the man. He was exactly the opposite of what she was afraid he'd be like under what she feared was his 'official' benevolent surface. Genuinely 'countryish,' almost primitive, like old mansard roofs and turrets and cobblestone streets, old women, old bikes, old babushkas. Then suddenly getting serious, lowering his voice, bending toward her as if there really were inquisitorial microphones somewhere in the room.

"May I be honest with you? No offence intended. But there's something about you that encourages 'confession,' confiding in. Jews are a lot less 'defensive' about themselves, aren't they? Not afraid to be themselves..."

"Maybe. I think that in general being in a Jewish community, you know, Hebrew school, Bar and Bat Mitzvahs, the bread and wine rituals before dinner, always a couple of old grandmothers and grandfathers around whose only function seems to be to be dripping with benevolence ... the more 'structure' you have, the more relaxed you get later on."

"Interesting, interesting. Well, I'll tell you, when you get to my age, especially if you've been reading books by this American author, Richard Morris, about the origin of the universe and all, everything just 'happening,' big bangs and all that ... I have a fatal habit of reading books on cosmology and the like before I go to bed. So that if I ever *do* get to sleep, after some skullcap and melatonin, all I ever dream about is universes beginning and ending ... although if there can't be an eternal God, how can there be an eternal universe? Or, on the other hand, how can the universe just appear out of nothingness?"

She shook her head. Confused. This wasn't what she expected. She'd expected to walk up the broad steps of orthodoxy into an eternal cathedral (beatitude) in the sky, not come face to face with more 'doubt' than she herself had ever had in her life.

"I'm confusing you, right?"

"Well… I didn't expect…"

"Neither did I! There I was, this little guy in parochial schools from first grade on, nuns and priests and all that, *in nomine patris, et filii et spiritus sancti*, back in catacomb times, practically. It all sounded OK to me, heaven up there somewhere in the clouds, the Christ you see depicted all over the cathedrals, sitting on His throne overlooking The Blessed, the Holy Spirit dove, God the Father, the Virgin … and eternal total joy, beatitude … that's what you want to hear, *n'est ce pas*? I guess I read too much, too much history of the church, all the councils, the fathers of the church, St. Augustine, Tertullian … or was he a Roman poet … a little bit of dementia, Roman poets and Roman saints … and then they got rid of Latin, that was a big mistake, got rid of Limbo … just decided that it was a 'mistake.'"

"Limbo?" she asked. She'd seen the word somewhere in her readings, but…

"When you weren't baptized, even though you were a good person, you couldn't go to heaven, so you went to limbo, which wasn't a place of beatitude, exactly, but no pain either, spent eternity in a kind of deep freeze, a pleasant deep freeze, or maybe like in one of Renoir's outside restaurant paintings, eternal summer with a little cognac in your hand, but not the full-fledged perfection of beatitude, beatitude, beatitude."

"So you're no longer a believer?"

Understanding him, but the language at times got a little difficult. Got the general ideas, but would have liked to have had a notebook and ask him about the words she hadn't got, wanted to eventually totally dominate *la langue français*.

"Put it this way, I want to believe, I force myself to believe, when I give communion I force myself to believe in transubstantiation."

"Transub…?"

"The 'real' presence, that the wine is Christ's blood, the host/bread is really Christ's body, that we're drinking Christ's blood and eating His body …"

She shuddered, a sudden chill. Shouldn't say what she was going to say, but …

"That sounds like cannibalism."

"It does, it does. But I 'believe' it, believe it all, the virgin birth, the trinity. It may sound like Jupiter and Juno, Hermes, Aphrodite, Hermaphrodite … or Quetzalcoatl or Viracocha …or…"

"You're losing me, Quetzalcoatl…?"

"Aztec god. Viracocha an Andean god associated with Tiawanaku in Bolivia. I spent a couple of years in Mexico and South America. In fact *the* single most beautiful time in my life was on a bus ride down from the Andes to the Chilean coast, snow-capped peaks and then lush valleys, rivers, forests, there was one Peruvian archaeologist who spent his entire life exploring the montaña in Peru, the area between the mountains and coast, and he found endless tombs and altars and … talk about sacred territory … the 'home of the gods.'"

"Home of the gods?"

"In ancient times they were always talking about going across the ocean from, say, the Middle East, going to the Home of the Gods. In the Sumerian epic, *Gilgamesh*, for example, across the ocean to Anaku, the Home of the Gods, where the thorn apples of immortality grew. Anaku. Tiawanaku. What do you think?"

"I'm lost. You sound more like an archaeologist than a priest…"

Peguy getting up, starting to pace around, 'disturbed' now, almost in tears.

"When you get to my age … 83 … maybe they should just retire us. Maybe I should start walking around going da-da-da-da all day, give in to my dementia. But I'm haunted day and night. My parents. Wanting them back so that I can talk to them again, make the bad things right. Toward the end, they were in Nantes, I was in Paris, the Andes. Distance, distance, distance. The same with my grandmother. Loved ones to hug again, a little kiss. That would be heaven for me, to walk through a door of clouds into a family dinner … green beans and artichokes, braised chicken and chocolate cake, demi-tasse cups of killer coffee. My old friends from the seminary. Friends and teachers. Parishioners I was particularly fond of, close to, gone, gone, gone. The children I baptized who are already dead. And they're all whispering to me 'Not much longer now, you're next…' Which I wouldn't mind if…" sitting back down, clasping his hands together, bending toward her, his face all desperate now, so much so that her strongest impulse was just to flee, get out while she still could, but instead forced herself to stay, listen, matching the intensity of his discourse with the intensity of her listening, "I wouldn't mind if … if I believed there was a cloud-door somewhere waiting for me to pass through, but what about AIDs, terrorism, earthquakes? Would I be surprised if some planet-sized rock suddenly appeared out of outer space and smashed the planet Earth to smithereens? And what's the point of death anyhow? Sea turtles live, what, three hundred years. For people you barely get started, are just getting used to Winter, Summer, Spring, Autumn, and, bang, you're gone. And where is Jesus now? Ascension into Heaven. OK. Or what about God the Father talking to Moses, why doesn't He appear again now and settle all this mess in Israel? The Jews are the 'promised people,' right? That's what the bible says. What about keeping His promise now that we're on the edge of The War of All Wars?"

Stopping, looking down at the floor.

While he'd been talking he was so full of life and vigour, more like twenty-five instead of eighty-three. Now it was as if he were about to die, was already dead … was one of the ghosts he'd been talking about.

What she'd wanted was some sort of quiet, calm believing priest who would lead her, not through the doorway of clouds, but the doorway of … what? Spines! Like Jesus' spiny crown … through spines into Enlightenment, all the prophecies fulfilled, finally acknowledging the Messiah who had been around already for more than two thousand years.

Now all she wanted to do was leave. He'd done such a beautiful job of stirring up her own deepest fears and despairs. No afterlives, hardly any life here.

Standing up.

"Well, I think I'd better…"

Holding out her hand. Only he didn't shake it.

"Five minutes more. That's all I ask. Five minutes more."

Hesitating. Mightn't it be better to just leave, break, if that's what it took, *break, break, break*, just get out, away, back into the sanity of falling leaves and bright sun, a little coffee, wind on her legs and through her hair…

Only she sat back down.

"Four minutes and thirty eight seconds."

"OK." Father Peguy suddenly becoming 'whole' again, calm, together, credible. "The reason I hang on to the Faith is that during my sleepless nights, in spite of all my herbs and pills, sometimes I begin to think of not just suicide in general, theoretical, but specifics, like jumping in front of a train, or getting some insecticide or something with arsenic in it and making myself a lethal cocktail, there are all sorts of books on poisons … and then Jesus comes in on a cloud 'Oh, ye of little faith, I am here, inside you, outside you, all around you, if only you *believe, believe, believe*,' so I believe, make an act of faith, God the Father, Son and Holy Spirit, the crucifixion and resurrection, the reward of heaven … everything, everything, everything … and I stretch out in my bed, my arthritis vanishes, I'm hardly a body at all, just pure spirit under sheets on the softest of beds, surrounded by the dead who never die … died … but just went on to another life … the spirit of the catacombs, not mourning deaths, but celebrating eternity."

"I don't know, I…" Miriam suddenly getting up, feeling like she was fleeing from some sort of spiritual-emotional holocaust, all the things that she never wanted to think about, all the things she was forever trying to escape from, this feeling of being surrounded by endless, senseless mindless universes, her own life and the lives of everyone around her the same as the lives (and deaths) of fleas, ants, spiders, flowers, trees, cloud … *nuages, nuages, nuages*/clouds, clouds, clouds … what was that poem by Supervielle, *prisonniers des mirages*, prisoners of mirages … *mirages, nuages*, the mirage of clouds… "I really have to be going, my children…"

"Children. How many?"

"Two boys. My husband was killed by terrorists in Tel Aviv…" starting to tell her story, then just wanting to flee, get out, away, out into the swirl of autumn, something immediate, sensuous, something to bring her back into her senses, into sense, away from endless negative theory.

"I'm so sorry." Peguy up, looking like he wanted to forcibly stop her from leaving, desperately sad, almost tears in his eyes, "I really should find an old people's home for goofy priests somewhere in Provence, lots of garden and river and sun … sit, sit, sit, sit … and wait to fade away into whatever we fade into…"

More and more and more.

"*Au revoir.*"

Distantly shaking hands with him.

He may have been eighty-three but he still looked vigorous, must have walked a lot, played tennis, exercise bicycle … something … you don't stay in that sort of condition just automatically.

Out of the office, past the nun in the outer office.

"*Salut!*"

A wave … and she was out into the bright sun, understanding why the ancients worshipped the sun, father sun, mother earth, sanely Zen buddhistically in the here and now, wishing there were some sort of Here and Now pills she could take to keep herself out of the cloudy labyrinths of her head, practically talking to the sky, *Shalom Ra, Adonai Elohainu, Adonai Echod / Give us peace, God, God, One God …* whatever His/Her name. One time when she was growing up in Tel Aviv, during services she'd had to sit with the other women in a special place at the back of the synagogue, and wear a 'veil,' not exactly a veil … but the connection with the Muslims was there, everything male-centred … except with the Catholics suddenly you went back to the Magna Mater religions of the ancient Mediterranean, didn't you, all the cathedrals in France, almost all of them, huge monuments to the Virgin, Notre Dame of This, Notre Dame of That … the Great Mother behind everything … as if the whole universe were somehow created not *by,* but *out of* her … motherplasm … and the male somehow subordinated to her … even the Christ child, the son of God.

IV

A Friday afternoon, just finishing up her last Hebrew class at the *schul*, twenty pre-Bar and Bat-Mitzvah kids she really loved, and felt she was doing great things for, to actually give them contact with an authentic Israeli like herself, like taking them by the hand back into history itself ... almost...

"*Mas schlom ha*? How are you ... male ... *Mas schlom eck*? How are you ... female. I know it seems needlessly complicated, but it was very common to ancient languages."

When the door opened and Rabbi Frankel stuck his head in, a little embarrassed or fake-embarrassed, acting embarrassed, he was so good at that, wasn't he.

"Listen, when you're finished with class could you come into my office for a moment?"

"OK."

What now?

Gone as quickly as he'd appeared.

Suddenly feeling very tired. A long autumn week. Loving the cold, so glad she was in Paris and not in Israel or New York or Afghanistan ... cool summer all summer. The only thing she really resented were the hordes of tourists that crowded everything up. You could hardly get into the Louvre or have a cup of coffee in the Tuileries.

"OK, class ... let's stop here ... you've been excellent all week. Excellent. Many thanks. See you on Monday."

And they all suddenly erupted into exuberant noise.

Au revoir, au revoir...

Would love to have just stayed on in Enghein for services at the synagogue that night, but had to get back to Paris itself, pick up Adam and Michael over at Pierre Courbet's place where they usually spent the afternoons after school.

They didn't need any special Hebrew school. Not with her drenching them in Hebrew practically full time. It was a wonder that they'd learned any French at all. Michael had almost no accent, Adam a little more believable every day. Envious of them sometimes. The older you get the more 'rigid' everything becomes ... still sounded like she'd just got off the boat – oops – the plane, from Israel.

Put her little light wool black jacket on. Looking forward and not looking forward to winter, a Mediterranean-soul at heart, sometimes tempted to just go into her (rather) vast bank account and quit all this farce of 'earning a living,' move to Provence, the Mediterranean, go to Cádiz in Spain, for God's sake, and 'retire,' just 'be,' *chocolat, chocolat, chocolat*.

Down the hall to Rabbi Frankel's office.

The secretary smiling, just a bit 'charged,' the smile, as if to say "I understand it all", was really in on something, as if there were something to be in *on*.

"He's waiting for you."

Door ajar.

Walked in.

He looked up from a pile of books and papers that he was intensely involved with, actually pushed them away from himself as if to make a point.

"Just getting together some ideas for the High Holidays, feeling a little guilty. I don't really write or think out anything, mainly just lift from sources. Too many references. They've made it too easy."

"And you wanted to…?"

"Sit down … sit down," and as she sat down on this big plush chair in front of his desk, thinking that it was a 'disarming' chair, took you off your guard, got you into just a bit too receptive a mood, as he got all convoluted and tortured. "My wife … you know … she's down in Provence visiting this aunt of hers … who knows how long she'll stay, she's such a heat-bug, she ought to move to Calcutta. There used to be all kinds of synagogues/congregations in India as a matter of fact, you wouldn't believe the size of some of the synagogues I visited there … but…"

"So the Hindus are tolerant of Jews?"

"Were … oh, still are … I've kind of lost track … but what I was wondering was, how about going out to dinner with me. Bring the kids along if you want, although…"

"They're over at a friend's house … big place over by Notre Dame … they usually stay the night, then we go to *schul* on Saturday mornings together … they're just a phone-call away," taking her little Panasonic out of her roughish-looking leather purse, flourishing it, as if to prove she was up to date or something, then feeling guilty that she was so 'easy,' flowing whatever way he wanted her to flow without any resistance at all, wondering, in the back of her mind, not what he wanted, which was very obvious, but what *she herself* wanted, as if she'd been *waiting* for this invitation for all eternity.

"So, OK ... you want to do it?"

"Why not?"

And she dialled the Courbet house. Mrs Courbet (Fleur) answering.

"*C'est moi ...*"

"You don't even have to ask," said Fleur, "of course they can ... not only *can* but it would be a pleasure, your two and my two get along like they were all part of the same brood."

"OK ... good ... I'll pick them up in the morning then, about eight thirty ..."

"*Parfait*/perfect ... and sometime, maybe not tomorrow, but sometime ... maybe they could go to the synagogue with you ... a little transcultural experience. No, not 'transcultural,' I meant 'ecumenical.' What do you think?"

"Whatever ... a little of what you call 'Old Testament' never hurt anyone."

"And neither does St. Paul," Fleur laughed. "See you in the morning."

And that was it.

"Amazing things, those little phones. I should get one. I'm starting to feel like a hippopotamus ... no, I didn't mean that ... dinosaur ... I'm starting to feel like a dinosaur..." getting up, putting on his suit coat, looking more like a lawyer or banker than a Rabbi, Miriam in a way missing the fanatic long hair and all black outfits of the orthodox, but whatever... "That student Rabbi, Rabbi Eulenberg, is doing the services tonight, he likes me to be there in the back row taking notes, but ..."

"You get enough feedback from everyone don't you?"

"That's one thing I don't have to fish for, feedback..." opening the door for her, suddenly in some sort of rush, like he'd caught his fish and he had to cut it open and eviscerate it before it went sour or something.

Out to his car, a quick drive downtown to Le Provence restaurant, insisting "if it's OK with you," as she got out of the car.

"I'm just your slave, aren't I? Either I do what you want or it's back to Israel for me," she smiled as they went in and sat down, thinking about Dr Shakshuka's in Jaffa and the *shakshuka* itself, tomatoes and eggs … missing the couscous … and the pictures of monkeys all over the walls … or Mon Jardin in Tel Aviv with its Romanian kebabs and chicken … talk about *gourmandise…*

Missed the wildly 'romantic' food in Israel, full of *l'histoire, toujours l'histoire* always all the peoples who had passed across the land and somehow left their trace there, like travelling back to Babylon itself, that's how little she felt it had all changed. But here it was fine too. She didn't have to look long at the menu. The Aubergines a la Bohemienne were *parfait* for her…

"I never can make my mind up about anything…"

"You seem to do OK in some areas," she smirked.

Him looking a little embarrassed, looking back at the menu, in the process catching furtive glance at her slim ankles and (perpetual) black lycra tights.

"Whatever that means."

A little red wine, a mumbled "*Baruch ata Adonai Eloheinu melech ha'olam borei pri hagafen…*/Holy art thou God, God, king of the universe, who gave us the fruit of the wine…" and an exuberant clicking of glasses, "*Lach heim!*/To life!"

To life, life, life, hating being peri-menopausal, hating to ever think of herself as one of those old ladies in the synagogue with a cane, a limp, a bent-over back and an almost-smile frozen on her face, wanting to die before she ever got there, whatever death meant, skulls and bones or forever in heaven in some sort of total bliss…

"So what are you going to have?" he asked. "Mrs Pensive … you really are a Mrs Pensive, aren't you?"

"Total nerd. I should have been born a man."

"Maybe you were, for all I know," he laughed, looking (again) down at her legs. "So…" looking intensely at her menu.

"I didn't know we were on some sort of tight schedule," she complained, almost whining, wanting to whine, whine, whine, like a whining cat out in an alley somewhere, hungry and locked out at 3a.m. on a cold winter night.

The waiter coming over to them and although she knew the Rabbi expected her to tell him to come back again later, give her a bit more time, she unhesitatingly ordered "I'll have the Aubergines à la Bohemienne…"

Which caught David off guard.

"And you sir?" the waiter on the surface the soul of calm and patience, but a millimetre down, stern, hurried, at the same time bored.

"The same, I suppose."

"Very good," taking the menus away.

David suddenly embarrassed and confessional.

"Whatever Aubergines a la Bohemienne is!"

"Aubergine, tomatoes, aubergine, tomatoes … in layers … topped by cheese…"

"Sounds horrible. What I wouldn't do for a falafel sandwich."

"I had a kibe earlier, a guy on the street in Paris…"

"I never trust those street guys. What if one of them happens to be a terrorist?"

"You mean like the Philistines or Babylonians or the people of Jericho … the Jerichovians, I suppose you'd call them…"

"What are you getting at?"

"That Israel never belonged to the Jews in the first place," she smiled, thinking *This isn't the conversation he expected at all, is it, it was all supposed to be whispers and innuendos, a sensuous lavender fog slowly engulfing us in its irresistible fragrance*, "that from the beginning Israel was conquered territory."

"Well, that's true, but…"

"The 'promised land,' if you could destroy the people who were already there…"

"So how are the kids enjoying Paris?" shifting topics, thinking himself so clever, so 'in control.'

"They miss Jericho," she smiled, "and the Jerichovians…"

"You can't let that topic alone, can you?"

"Just kidding," she laughed, sat back, a little more wine, "I just like to get you going … you're so … rabbinical…"

Which he had to laugh at too.

A little more wine for him too.

"I thought maybe, after we eat, you might want to come over to my place. Not far from the casino. We could walk and see the swans. Your kids'll be all right?"

"They're fine. Mrs Courbet's husband is a banker … they have all this room … you know, it practically looks like Versailles … the mouldings and corbels and even pergolas in the mini-garden…"

"Corbels, pergolas?"

"Just 'things' … you know I've always been fascinated by architecture. The same way I'm fascinated by hills and valleys, untouched landscapes. In fact I could spent the rest of my life just skimming over southern France and Spain and England, Bohemia, a few houses here and there, mainly just bones buried here and there, the bones outnumbering the present-day inhabitants … ghosts, ghosts, ghosts…"

"I'll be honest with you," he said, lowering his voice, "I'm so horny that I can hardly write a sermon any more, much less worry about archaeology and ghosts…"

Miriam with her wine-glass to her lips, just beginning a sip, laughing, spraying her wine all over herself and the table, just a touch on him, quickly wiping everything up with her napkin.

"Sorry … that was the last thing I expected to hear. Only just tell me why?"

"I'm the one who should be sorry. I don't know…" sitting back, getting pensive and solemn. "It's just that she's such a … munchkin, gnome … and with a personality to match. And getting divorced … allowable, I suppose, but not for the model of uprightness and normality that I'm supposed to be … I don't run the congregation, I'm just an employee. You know how things work."

"You could always change careers, go to the US, somewhere else … or do something about her. I mean shape her up, a little surgery, beautification."

"If that's all it were, the physical. But it's a lot more than that. She's got so *bitter* about things. The same reason you left Israel. She's afraid the whole thing is going to spread here, especially if the French government starts getting anti-Arab. The irony being that all the Arabs I've ever known I've liked not just a little, but a lot. Lots of 'gusto,' life in them …"

The waiter bringing their dishes.

"Enjoy!"

Probably an 'Arab' himself, she thought, a Catholic Lebanese, smiling as the thought came to her. She was getting just a little too good at identifying where people came from, what language(s) they spoke; the week before had seen some blacks on the street and had asked them "Sudanese?" and they had reacted a bit scared, "But how do you know?" some Russians a couple of weeks back, Russians, but "Armenian Russians?" she'd asked them at the cash register of the grocery store, again surprised at her accuracy.

David poking at the little pile of melted cheese topped stuff on his plate.

"Smells great…"

"Garlic, aubergine, tomatoes, thyme, bay leaf, onions, Gruyère cheese … what do you want?"

"This, I guess," forking into it, started to cautiously chew, sitting back, a bit more wine, another Lach Heim, then lowering his face, "This … and you…"

"I don't think I should go over to your place at all. You're a little too unsubtle. Seduction is all about surprises, isn't it? You're too … gross, isn't that the word … gross…"

Unsure of her French, would have preferred to shift over into Hebrew, but then the whole evening would turn into a class, and if it were going to be a bit of a class (her French light years better than his Hebrew) she'd prefer being the student rather than the teacher.

"I can just leave, take my food home and liberate you from my presence altogether."

"The next thing you'll be doing is firing me!"

"I couldn't if I wanted to. Not that I do. It's all the Board of Directors, that Michael Bubner. He's originally from Israel, you know, big Mr Smiles … but under it all he's as tough as … I almost said this aubergine, but…"

"Seen any good movies recently?" she smiled as she called the waiter over.

"*Oui, Madame…*"

"How about a Salade Mechouia for me … for us both."

"Good idea."

And he was gone.

"Are all Israelis always 'in charge'? I'm not much for salads…"

"You'll love the Mechouia. We had a French cook in Israel. Before my husband's murder," stressing 'murder,' could have just said 'death,' but she didn't want to lose perspective, 'murder' it was and 'murder' it would always be, murder after murder after murder after murder, regardless of who was occupying who's territory.

"So you must have been doing very well …"

"Very well."

Tears coming involuntarily into her eyes as she remembered *just* how well they had been doing, the house just off the beach, the cars, the holidays to Europe and Japan and the US, Tampo-Boca Raton in winter almost interchangeable with Tel Aviv…

"And whatever prompted you to come to Paris?"

Stopping for a moment, looking out at the people walking by on the street outside, the whole sense of 'security' and 'peace' that she felt here…

"All the shit that has happened in Paris precludes the possibility of any more shit happening!"

Which got him laughing.

"Not necessarily. What about all the thousands of years of shit in Israel?"

"Well … it could have all ended if…"

"If…?"

The waiter appeared with the salad.

"That was quick," he said.

"We had it waiting for you," smiled the waiter putting the plates on the table, David sampling it.

"Very peppery…"

"A close cousin to Pepperonata."

"Pepperonata?"

"Italian."

"In that case…" digging into it, olives and parsley sprigs, red and yellow peppers, all drenched in olive oil and red wine vinegar, "I'd better watch out hanging around with you, I might just get healthy or something…"

"Wouldn't that be horrible?"

Then going back to his Aubergines a la Bohemienne, then sitting back.

"Two questions still unanswered ... why Paris? And how could the shit have ended in Israel?"

"OK, first Paris. I was here as a child. Sometimes we came here summers, my father bought me a pile of old poetry books, I got involved with French composers like Milhaud, Satie, Debussy. I play, or at least *played* piano, kind of fell in love with Debussy. What a way to die, colon cancer, but even while he was dying he was still writing beautiful, imagistic, impressionistic music, kind of a lesson in awareness, 'Here, here, here, concentrate on the Here and Now. Kind of Zen buddhistic. Not to mention Monet and Renoir, more of the same message, 'Catch the snow and the willows, drive through the country and love the hills and clouds, walk through the Parc Morceau and immerse yourself in the narcissuses and the grandifloras with their citronella scent, kiosks and roses, the Roman colonnades and Egyptian mini-pyramid, the grandeur of the fountains and stairways in the Parc de Saint Cloud. Israel is *older* and all that, but what they've preserved here is the chocolates and whipped cream of the past, not 'history' for the sake of history, but 'history' for the sake of its surviving gems..."

Stopping, choking up, taking a drink of wine, stopping and just wanting to go 'out,' out, out, out into the parks, a drive to Monet's place, where he spent his last years standing painting flower by flower as if his life depended on it ... and maybe it (buddhistically) did.

"Of course I was born here, parents from Morocco ... but you sound like a tourist guide."

Which she didn't appreciate at all, felt like simply getting up and walking out, leaving her half-finished food behind.

More wine, thinking that if she hung about him long enough she'd become an alcoholic, just to blur and blot out the sarcasms and quips.

"Maybe I should go on a tour right now!"

Starting to get up.

"No, no, no ... I'm sorry ... I'm such a..."

"You are indeed!"

Having to laugh, sitting back down, nibbling on a piece of aubergine.

"But what could have been done to stop the current situation in Israel?"

"I have an even more radical view of Muslims than you. The ones I've known, and I've known plenty, were always the soul of graciousness to me. Only if you invade someone's territory, start 'colonizing' where there's barely room to survive anyhow … there's that whole business of 'territorial imperatives,' isn't there?"

"Right, there is … but now…?"

"*Ça suffit, n'est ce pas?* / That's enough, OK?"

"OK."

"Have you ever been to Giverny?"

"Giverny…?"

"Where Monet spent his last years. Beautiful, the way they've reconstructed it. You can practically feel his presence there. In fact I was going to write a book about the old impressionists. Title: *Surviving*. How to go into old age gracefully…"

"You're hardly old enough for that!" he laughed, looking down at her legs again.

And, quite honestly, she hadn't felt so 'hot' for years, asking herself *What was the point of being if you weren't being yourself, so many months of 'fasting,' for what exactly … thou shalt not …* thou shalt not what … BE, SIMPLY BE, LIKE A BEE…

"Getting there. Peri-Let's-Not-Get-Into-It…"

"Not Peri-anything, except maybe Persephone."

"Persephone?"

"The Greek personification of Spring."

Pushing away his plates. Just slightly. Delicately.

"*Basta!* Enough for me…"

Her adopting her mother's harpy tone for a minute.

"I want you to eat every last bit of food on those plates. There are people starving all over the world!"

Which got him laughing.

"I could see you on the big screen. Really! Bette Davis!"

"Bette Davis?"

"So you're not into old films? That's practically all I watch … old Israel, old films, old, old, old … I look into the mirror these days and begin to see my father…"

Patting himself on his (slight) paunch.

"And me my mother … just a bit too much of my father…"

Pushing his chair out.

"So shall we…?"

"No dessert?"

"*Plus tard* / Later."

Giving her wry little evil smile.

Of course she was supposed to say "Not me, my friend, time for me to trundle back home…"

Only to whose home?

Helping her on with her little black jacket, her wanting, wanting, wanting *so much* for him to just grab her then and there and do his/their thing. So many years of daily sex and now months and months without it, always feeling guilty and dirty if she *serviced* herself. And it never was the same, not just physical but a sharing of selves, spirit intertwining with spirit, as if anyone just *alone* was necessarily incomplete, we were *made* to be spliced together, *bone of my bone, flesh of my flesh, and she shall be called Woman because she was taken out of man … and they shall cleave unto each other and become one flesh*, as if fucking were a kind of return to earlier stages of creation … not quite sure about the implied subordination of Woman to Man, Female to Male, but…

"Don't you love this time of year, the leaves just beginning to turn, a breath of cold by night, bright sunny days … my boys sleep like stones in this kind of weather."

"I don't know if I like the sound of 'sleep like stones,'" he smiled as he opened the car door for her, an old Mercedes, always saying he'd rather have an old diamond than a new piece of glass, kind of obsessed by antiques, every time she'd gone to his house for Passover amazed at the over-abundance of things … clutter … but a museumish clutter that you slowly not only got used to, but began to long for … imitate.

Just a short ride over to his place, an older brick house, slate roof, stone columns on both sides of the elaborate brick staircase, a house that said "Not quite regal, but very much 'inside.'" Inside what? Some ineffable, beyond-words sense of having 'made it.'

Two books of his out about the bible/biblical times, the bible applied to the modern world. Not that they sold very well, not that he was rich or anything, but …

Into the antiquish living room, a thousand questions she wanted to ask about the menorahs, paintings, spearpoints in little framed boxes, even a collection of Buddha statues filling one wall.

"How about some sorbet? I've got apricot, peach, raspberry … you name it … and a little brownie … there's this bakery down at the corner … an old woman from Provence, in fact. Sometimes I feel like I'm invaded by Provence, that I should move down there when I retire. No Arab accent, right? You don't hear any accent, do you?"

"Not at all. Should I?"

"Well, my parents used to speak Arabic at home when I was a kid, even when we got here. And shop at Arab markets. A little Yiddish thrown in at home …"

Laughing, although she felt that maybe she shouldn't, starting to sit down on a big leather sofa in the living room, a sofa that looked kind of out of place in Antique-World … looking to him for 'permission'.

"Sit! Sit! I'll bring the goodies in here … your flavour?"

"You decide. Pretend you're on Sinai and listen to God."

Which he didn't laugh at, just a touch of chagrin on his pussycat face, then forcing a quick smile and disappearing through the dining room and its elaborate antiquish table and chairs back into the kitchen, her eyes trailing across the pictures on the walls, paintings and poetry, one fragment of what looked like a fifteenth century tapestry, the collection of old, old menorahs on the shelf above the what looked like marble fireplace, asking herself why she had stuck herself and her two boys into such a pipsqueak of an apartment when she could have easily afforded this much and even more, then the answer coming back at her out of the deepest depths of her mind, "The future … you won't always be around … the future … the boys turned men, their college educations, plus, plus, plus, plus…"

Which was true enough, *n'est ce pas*?

Although, if all you ever did was plan for the future it was as if were you already dead ... and wasn't her whole philosophy beginning to be an immersion in the glorious, impressionistic NOW?

Running her hand over the light brown suede surface of the sofa. *Joli, joli, joli* ... beautiful, beautiful, beautiful...

As he came back into the room, a bundle of energy, carrying a large gold-painted wooden tray that looked three-hundred years old, with some antiquish Japanese (?) dishes on it, the brownies on plates, the sorbet in bowls, the pottery (which was how she saw it, not as ordinary dishes, but 'pottery,' like something in the Louvre) grey, artfully painted with deep green bamboo.

"You wouldn't want some coffee ... or ..."

"Tea, right?"

"Well ... deep down I guess I'm an old samurai at heart."

"Old samurai, old furniture, old dishware, you're a real antiquity, aren't you? Where did you get all this–"

"Junk, right? Well, I haunt flea markets, not just in Paris but ... remember last year when I went to Lisbon? I rented a car, found out about flea markets, went up into the mountains ... there was a place, I forget the name."

Miriam putting down her dishes for a moment, taking a framed ceramic from the wall next to her, David visibly disturbed by her taking it off the wall.

"OK, I'll put it back on!"

"I didn't say anything..."

"Your face talks all by itself."

Coming over to her, taking it out of her hand and re-hanging it.

"Tricky, re-hanging these things..."

A drawing on it of the front of Notre Dame. Only there was a market in front of the cathedral. Unheard of! And no cars, just horse-drawn carriages.

"How come the carriages, no cars?"

"Well, Renoir, you know, before he began painting worked in a ceramics factory in Sevres, I think it was. It's not signed, but if you study it closely. *I* think it's a Renoir drawing."

"Which, of course, you can't prove, but..."

"Maybe you can prove it. If you get other known Renoir ceramics and compare them…"

"But which you're not doing?"

"Am doing. Slowly, slowly, everything slowly. Like the Spanish say *poco a poco se va lejos* / little by little goes a long way. I try to do everything that way, pieces, like pyramids…"

Suddenly *touched* by him and, what was it, his innocence, ingenuousness, honesty. Tears in her eyes. Which she was ashamed of.

"Everything OK?"

"You're not supposed to notice."

"But what? Something I said…?"

"It's only been a few years since, you know … my tragedy … but it seems like centuries. Sometimes I walk around in Paris feeling like I've been here for centuries, that the king is still in Versailles, the revolution is still centuries off, the Germans taking over Paris, that I'm liable to run into St. Thomas Aquinas walking somewhere in the Bois du Boulogne … I could just as well be on peyote or kava kava … but the strongest thing I take is espresso coffee."

"But that's not what you really want to say, is it?"

Surprised at his intuitiveness … depth.

"What I really want to say is…" taking a big bite out of the brownie, tasting like cacao-beans, just off the bush, it was that fresh, *primitive*… "that the brownies are delicious."

"Still playing games…"

"Maybe I should just leave."

"First finish your sorbet and brownie," he answered playfully, not taking her solemnly; seriously yes, but not solemnly.

Digging into her sorbet, a mixture of orange, raspberry and, she guessed, cherry, all three delicious.

Things she never bought, or seldom, like sorbet, all sorts of gustatory treats swimming around her like dolphins, and so much of the time she stayed just dull, dull, dull … more visual that taste-oriented … always keeping sex out of her mind, as if she were the buddha or something…

But now…

Finished all she wanted, put her dish back down on the

table and got up.

"You're not really leaving?"

Wanting to say *No, not ever, I'm the paint on the walls, the varnish on the floors, light fixtures and window-trims* ... just standing there, as he came over and, instead of backing off, walking away, she put her arms out and he did the same, the two of them coming together like lobsters making love.

"*Je voudrais dire 'jamais,' 'jamais,' 'jamais.'* / I would like to say never, never never."

"So say it. My wife and I..."

"Was she ever pretty?"

"Never. I married her because. Well, she seemed so 'safe', 'permanent' ... and she has been that, but ... do you want to...?"

"You don't ask, you pick up the signals."

"Me-nerd and her-nerd, that's why we got together, she has this degree in physics, and..."

Pushing him in toward the stairway now, bedrooms upstairs, not at all subtle, feeling this tremendous bestial, basic, primal urge now. She was a bitch in heat, wasn't she, harts, hounds, butterflies, flies, dolphins, all we were really on the earth for was to reproduce ourselves, just like the flowers and trees and everything else, the only thing that really made any sense...

"I really should take a shower first."

"Take a long walk on a short pier!"

Going upstairs alone, loving the old carved oak bannister, the stained-glass light over the stairway, thinking she should have been (should be!) an architect, restorer of old houses, creator of new-old houses, in the real-estate business...

Finding the master bedroom and the huge canopied bed.

Just what you'd expect.

The little gold-wood dressing table off to the side of the bed. Taking off her clothes, getting under the covers, like peeling a banana, really, peeling an orange, wondering how she had the nerve, cheek, shamelessness, Jerko David coming in surprised, as if he still didn't get the idea, then pulling the long, tapestry drapes closed, as if he were afraid that God might see him through the windows, *Baruch ata Adonai Eloheinu melech*

Ha'olam / Holy Art Thou God, God, King of the Universe …
wanting, always wanting to believe that God *was* king of the
universe, that there was a Someone out there in control, that it
wasn't all freaky chance. And making it most of the time. But
then Vesuvius would erupt or some virus would kill off
thousands or … even the situation in Israel. God always *there*,
present, talking in ancient times, whatever happened to Him
since TV was invented?

David taking his clothes off, half behind a drape.

Ashamed.

Although he didn't have that much to be ashamed about,
his body wasn't *that* bad, although she wondered what was
supposed to be sexually triggering about human bodies
anyhow? She never got turned on by gazelles or deer or
orangutans in the zoo, and how were we *really* different from
the rest of the animal kingdom …

"Don't be so … *afraid* !" she laughed, "I've been to the zoo
lots of times…"

"It's just that…"

"Just that what, thou shalt not commit adultery?"

"Well…" his trousers off already, a little tummy, but big
deal, starting to unbutton his shirt, stopping, starting to
rebutton it, "Maybe you're right, there isn't a lot of ambiguity in
the rule book, is there…"

"I'm all hot!" she bitched, beyond commandments and
talmuds and kabbalahs now, just a wild animal out in the
jungle somewhere waiting to be fucked, no rules just smells
and glands and needs, and if she got pregnant again, so be it,
that's what it was all about, wasn't it, penises and clitori and
hormonal drives, driving the whole world toward simply
reproduction, life, life, life, from Queen Anne's lace and
papayas to mountain gorillas and flies.

"I'm sorry, but…"

Taking his trousers and socks and shoes and slipping
guiltily out of the room, her wanting to scream at him "So sin
already! That's what it's all about, sin and repentance, the rules
are there just to be broken now and then…" Not Thou Shalt
Not Kill, which was unbreakable, but coveting your neighbour's
wife (or husband?) or a little bribe now and then? Was she,

45

were *they* still alive, or just Buddha-faced icons painted on a sanctuary wall somewhere, gold haloes and sinless.

She didn't want to be sinless.

Reached down and began to touch herself, imagining her dead husband for a moment. Now there was a real *beast*, and it was so great to be bestial with him.

He'd been so big and athletic (soccer), hot, hungry, wanting it twice a day most of the time. Why not? Like having beer and barbecue twice a day, turning it all into just times between ecstasies, their two ecstatic wrestling matches in the morning and evening the centres of her day, everything else in between either relaxation or anticipation.

But then he was gone, it was just cemeteries and funeral services and emptiness, as if some huge theatrical lighting switch had been pulled down backstage, and voice had shouted "Go home, everyone, the show is cancelled, no more show tonight…"

Cold, dead, part of her in the grave with him already.

Getting up, getting dressed, as if she didn't have a body at all. Going into the bathroom and combing her hair with a brush filled with David's wife's hair. Big deal.

A little lipstick retouching up.

She looked so young. Maybe it was the lighting. Sometimes she'd go into the cloakroom in a restaurant and look in the mirror and she'd look like her own grandmother, but here she could have been seventeen instead of forty-four.

Maybe it was the hormones, the frustration itself.

Frustration pills. One a day and lose a day of age every day, one year younger every year.

Wouldn't even want that. If Death had walked in the door, she would have embraced him.

Mort and Death merging in her mind.

Mort hadn't been embalmed, so probably all the flesh was gone already, although in the desert you never knew … imagining his flesh all dried out and stretched around his skull. Prominent supra-orbital ridge, almost neanderthal. Imagining that … and his dead, dried-up eyes staring up at her.

Starting to cry.

"Jesus!" coming out of her involuntarily, "Jesus, sweet Jesus!"

Hurrying down the stairs, David in the living room smoking a pipe. Like Sherlock Holmes, for God's sake. A dressing gown on. Reading a newspaper. As if nothing at all had happened. No crises in his life.

"You don't have to…" he started in, getting up.

"Yes I do!"

Out the door into the surprisingly chilly night. Needed more than her little black jacket tonight. But loved winter here too …loved it all, the black (and not black) Arabs, the poor white-trash-ish neighbourhoods, the whores and druggies, all set down in an historical setting that whispered *Où sont les rois, la noblesse?* / Where are the kings, the nobility?

A cab passing by that she hailed.

Down to the train station. Tempted to just take a taxi all the way back to Paris, but liked to keep at least the surface appearance of thrift, and financial carefulness, you never knew *when/if* her whole fortune might evaporate, American airlines going into bankruptcy, all the corporate corruption. Maybe she should stop watching the evening news altogether, go into her room and sit on the floor and cross her legs and become the Buddha. The *real* Buddha, not his orientalized icon. Where had she seen the drawing of the *real* (Indian Indian) Buddha? The Metropolitan Museum in NY? Or had it been the Louvre?

Off at the train station, a generous tip to the cabbie who smiled back generously, always feeling sorry for the 'lower classes,' a bit of a communist in her, *n'est ce pas*? It was a good theory anyhow, wasn't it … total equality…

Lucky to catch a train in just a few moments, as she sat there watching the suburbs slide by still feeling very sensuous, sexual, more seventeenish than forty-three-ish.

Should get on her cellular phone and call her kids, take them back home with her, but they were all right where they were, and she somehow wanted to be alone, alone, alone, *toute seule,* loving the feel of her legs in their tight lycra, the feeling of her ample breasts encased in their black lace cups, feeling like she was becoming a crow in heat, a wolf somewhere out on the tundra screaming to be fucked, amused at her sexuality, amazed that it had nothing to do with David or anyone else, just her involved with herself, when she got back to the apartment getting out of the lift and opening the door, taking a quick piss, then taking off all her clothes but her tights, putting on some black suede ankle-strap shoes that she could hardly walk in but certainly could lie down in, slipping into a soft black lace peignoir and lying down on her bed, pillows piled so she could kind of sit up, began to touch herself 'down there,' clitoris and into the vagina itself, all the time looking at her legs, playing with her nipples, unexpectedly thinking about something she'd read in one of the books she'd bought about Catholicism, about the sin of masturbation, bypassing the natural purpose of things, sperms that were supposed to become babies never having a chance to travel to any eggs ... but her playing with herself didn't waste eggs ... it was just pure joy, *me, myself and I.*

Maybe that was the only relationship she was capable of any more, the various fragments of her self coming together for a little fun and becoming non-trinitarianly ONE.

V

It was a funny way to 'make love,' establish contact … whatever … but a week after their making-love farce, David came into Miriam's Hebrew class, just three minutes before let-out time, and she told her *gang*, "OK, everybody, that's it. But how about a hello to Rabbi Frankel?"

And almost in unison they sang out an ebullient "*Salut!*" mixed in with a few "*Bonjours*," and "*Ça vas?*" Once they were gone Frankel coming in and very awkwardly and uncomfortably sitting on the desk.

"I was wondering if, this Shabbat, you might want to read the Torah portion for us … your Hebrew. You know, it's so authentic, guttural, 'ancient,' the real thing…"

"OK … it doesn't hurt to have a little of the 'real thing.'"

Double-thinking, 'real thing,' real accent … real sex … Still feeling very strongly for him, even his childish awkwardness attractive to her, his ugly dwarf wife back now, which seemed to build a big bird-cage around him, and there he was inside cheeping, "Cheep, cheep, cheep…" like a baby canary.

And if he were a canary, what was she, a vulture?

OK. Why not! Feeling like swooping down on him and almost literally devouring him … as she started to recite the next Shabbath's Torah portion in Hebrew (Genesis, Chapter 12): "Now the Lord had said unto Abraham 'Get thee out of thy country, and from thy kindred, and from thy father's house, unto a land that I will show you…'"

Really throwing David for a loop.

"But how did you know that…?"

"I have a calendar."

Pointing to the calendar on the wall next to the blackboard.

"But still … I'm impressed. If you'd just asked me what I'd asked you, I still would have had to check it out. And I'm the Rabbi, after all…"

"Pardon me for stepping into your territory," getting up and coming over to him (now that all the kids were gone) and giving him a hug and kiss, "Even if your gnome-wife is back…"

Smiling.

"She is that."

Sitting on the desk next to him as he put his arm around her as if to stop her from falling.

Maybe time for a little confessing.

"Sometimes at night, you know the TV gets a bit much, my rented films, the boys are in bed, I've got another copy of the same calendar at home. I am an Israeli, after all … and Chapter 12 of Genesis in a way is the beginning of all our problems…"

David looking *very* perplexed now.

"The beginning of all our problems?"

"God showing Abraham the plain of Moreh and saying 'Unto thy seed will I give this land…' Combine that with 'I will make thee a great nation, and I will bless thee … and I will bless them that bless thee, and curse him that curseth thee … and in thee shall all families of the earth be blessed…' not to mention the little footnote about the land being already in the possession of the Canaanites: 'And the Canaanite *was* then in the land.' So He is giving Abraham somebody else's land, *nicht wahr?*"

"Please, no *nicht wahr*, no German, I mean none, none, none … *s'il vous plaît* … my skin begins to creep and my hair curl…"

"You certainly don't need any more hair-curling," she smiled and ruffled up his already super-curly hair. David looking around to be sure no one saw her, actually a touch of blushing in his cheeks. "You really are a prude, aren't you?"

"It's a job, isn't it?" tensing up, getting up from the desk, "Maybe I can just do the Torah reading myself, have Cantor Katz do it … the usual…"

"No," she protested, pulling him back, loving his tweed (Harris, the genuine thing?) jacket that kept whispering to her *Autumn, Autumn, Autumn, almost Winter now*, "I want to do it … I want to do … everything…"

"I wouldn't think so," answering petulantly and peeved, "not from the way you acted the other day."

Her suddenly shifting back to Genesis, hating defrosting old soup or sushi, feeling she was back in school in Israel about to get chastised from misbehaviour. She'd done what she'd done what she'd done…

"You don't really believe God went around giving somebody else's property to Abraham. And couldn't you say that the

50

Palestinians are the descendents of the Canaanites, just trying to get back what lawfully belongs to them?"

"You're starting to sound like a Palestinian yourself, you know that? What's going on?"

"Do you really believe that God created the heavens and the earth and the earth was without form and void and darkness was upon the face of the deep and God said 'Let there be light!' and light appeared? So you really think there's some eternal Somebody out there capable of creating universes?"

"What's got into you?"

"Eternal universe, eternal God. If He would only reappear now, appear on TV, the internet … but all we have is silence, silence, silence … and chaos…"

"Really, what's got into you?"

"Too much talking to Father Peguy?"

"Father Peguy?"

"He's a priest over at Notre Dame cathedral. Kind of oldish, cynical, too much reading, too much thinking, turning into a questioner, doubter, if not a downright disbeliever."

"What are you talking to him for? What's going on?"

"I don't know, I started going to Notre Dame every day, drawing the stone sculptures of Jesus, the Virgin, the saints … getting books on Catholicism … falling in love with the idea of the Messiah having already come, and we just didn't 'get it.'"

"We just didn't 'get it'? Jews for Jesus…"

"More than that. Ex-Jews … *in nomine Patris, Filii et Spiritus Sancti…*"

"The Father, Son and Holy Spirit."

"I'm surprised you know that."

"You'd be surprised about a lot of things about me, if you'd just give yourself a chance," he smiled unexpectedly, reaching over and touching her hair, not looking to see if anyone was around. "So you don't want to do the Torah reading?"

"I'll do it. Happily. Once a Jew always a Jew. Like Jesus. 'Holy, holy, holy.' *Qadosh, qadosh, qadosh*, where do you think the Christians get their Mass from? Holy, holy, holy, and the bread and wine of Passover becoming the Body and Blood of Christ … and the Virgin Mary and the Magna Mater…"

"Magna Mater?"

"The Great Mother. Pre-Jewish middle-easternisms, mediterraneanisms…"

"Whatever happened to my simple little Eve?"

"Whatever happened to my simple little Adam?"

Into each others' arms now, they could have been in the coliseum in ancient Rome and it wouldn't have made any difference, let the birds chirp and the ducks quack, Miriam for a moment feeling like they *were* Adam and Eve in the original Garden of Eden, just one inch away from cleaving to each other forever and forever … totally unashamed…

Genesis. Chapter 2.

Talk about getting back to beginnings.

Then him pulling away, Eden becoming just a classroom in the synagogue again, a job, a job, a job.

"See you in the morning, then…"

And he was gone. His turn.

The next morning Miriam very happily mounted the bima/ altar and sat down next to the Rabbi and Cantor, thinking how 'different' she was from the rest of the women in the congregation who were still sitting in the back of the synagogue wearing scarves, not exactly 'veils,' not exactly Muslim … but almost…

The usual Saturday morning crowd, Kurt Horwitz, who had actually spent part of his childhood in a concentration camp in Germany, Auschwitz, she vaguely remembered, not that she came that often on Saturday mornings … next to him his 'converted' wife, looking very Flemish/Belgian, fattish, always smiling or on the edge of smiling, kind of a latter day female Buddha, in front of her Jacob Boehme, who had a shoe store in Engheim no big deal, but looking very good at, what was he, eighty-one, wishing she could make it to eighty-one, eighty-five, even more, stand on the hills and look down on it, back at it all, her two boys married, her life full of grandchildren … Dr Stein and his wife Sarah, maybe in their seventies, Sarah his second wife, overdone earrings, overdone dyed hair and plastic surgery but pulling it off, hard to say she wasn't what she tried to look like – somewhere around forty-five…

And then next to her…

Wait, wait, wait … it couldn't be. This little old guy in a dark suit with a purple skullcap perched on top of what was left of his white hair. Looking very much at home. Father Peguy. What was he doing here?

A strong impulse to go down and confront him. Almost a smirk on his face. He *couldn't* have known that she was going to read the Torah portion. David couldn't have/wouldn't have called him after she'd told him she'd been seeing him! Which meant that Peguy usually came on Shabbath mornings? Who was converting who?

The Rabbi (David) beginning the service…

"How lovely are your tents, O Jacob, your dwelling-places, O Israel…"

His Hebrew *good* but she missed the *authentic* gutturalness of it all, missed Israel, missed the sea, missed the sense of history that was so much her own personal thing, like her skin, her hair … thinking 'skin,' 'hair' and suddenly facing Death as if He were there with scythe in hand, a skeleton wearing a long black, head-covering cloak, standing in front of her, whispering "Not long now, however long, still not LONG!" Thinking of her dead parents, dead husband, dead aunts and uncles, dead, dead, dead…

Not long now.

Peguy. Was he winking at her? Smiling and winking?

Oh, God…

Only *which* God?

Ignoring him. Very consciously ignoring him. During the whole service. And then, when it was her turn to read the Torah portion, getting up, almost tripping, her heels a little too high, should have worn flats, looked down at the carpet for a moment and then when she looked up, intending to read the Torah portion directly at Peguy, guttural it out, spit it out, back to primitive Hebrew, out in the desert defying the sands … only *merde!* he wasn't there…

Vanished.

For a moment questioning her own sanity. Was she hallucinating or…?

Hesitating a bit too long, David clearing his throat.

And then launching off into her thick, guttural Israeli

Hebrew, loving it, going back, back, back to the beginning, God giving Canaan to Abraham, then the famine, and Abraham going into Egypt to survive, then the confusing problems with Sarah and Pharaoh and Abraham, then the problems with Lot, then God giving Abraham all the land he could see, "And I will make thy seed as the dust of the earth, so that if a man can number the pieces of dust of the earth, then shall thy seed also be numbered..." to hell with Bera, the king of Sodom, Birsha, the king of Gomorrah, Shinab, king of Admah, Shemeber, king of Zebolim, Zoar, the king of Bela ... as if they didn't exist.

But still loving to be Israeli, loving to be identified as such, feeling ancient herself, feeling God talking to her, giving her all this land, giving her all this future, invincible, touched by the Divine, Elohainu, Adonai ... echad ... always echad, echad, echad ... one, one, one ... no trinities or blessed virgins.

Afterwards, at the Oneg party, David congratulating her:

"What a reading. It wasn't just a reading but a performance. I don't know, you took me back, back, back, back to beginnings, like I'd never been taken back before."

"That's just what was happening to me. We were on the same wavelength," she answered, for a moment feeling totally cemented to him, one body, one flesh, even with two feet between them at the table as they munched on their cookies and cheesecake, missing all the old traditional Jewish things they'd had at Onegs after services when she was growing up ... even forgetting the names ... but still remembering the flavours. Hamantaschen ... little folded back on themselves cookie-cakes.

Old Mrs Greenberg, half crippled, but still very well 'kept up,' fashionable, with her slim ankles and diamond earrings and beautiful pure white, silverish hair, coming up and embracing her.

"Beautiful job. You ought to be up on the bima a lot, lot more..."

"A lot more!"

Abraham, her husband, with this brace holding up his head, his whole neck just 'gone,' baggy-eyed, low-voiced, but still heroically at Saturday morning services. Giving her a hug too. Feeling very much at home, at home, at home, almost as if she'd never left Israel at all.

The next evening , putting her boys, Adam and Michael, in bed, ten o'clock, after a day in the Bois de Boulogne and then a long evening of video games and TV, good boys, Adam and Michael, both of them looking uncannily like her dead husband. So much so that sometimes she didn't even want to look at them too closely, not wanting that whole complex of memories to be revived, too many days at the beach, too many coffees, too much falafel, too much sex … although, it was weird, she was only forty-four and she had managed to just turn off sex … except when she was close to David, for a moment, as she got up to close the shutters on the windows of their bedroom, wishing that David's red dwarf wife would just die already, vanish, dust in the winds … horrible, sinful thought, too soon after Rosh Ha-Shanah and Yom Kippur, repentance, a clean road for the new year…

Closing the shutters when her eye was caught by someone across the street down below, under the streetlight, a little old man with white hair in a long rain-coat/overcoat kind of thing, staring up at her.

It couldn't be.

But it was…

Father Peguy.

Terrified for a brief knifeflash of a moment, but then feeling almost sad for the poor old guy, that he didn't have anything else to do but 'pursue' her. Then amazed at how well he was doing it.

Closing the shutters with almost a bang, much more forcefully than usual, bending over her boys bathed in the soft bedlights next to their beds. Calm, calm, calm…

"What's going on?" asks Adam, eyes half-open, very tired after their long, long walk in the Bois de Boulogne this afternoon, not enough for her, never enough for her, but too much for them, thinking of them as little babies, realizing that she'd *always* think of them as her little babies, that's what mothers do, isn't it, no one ever grows up or ages, and then Death comes with his scythe and whop! adieu, adieu, adieu…

"Nothing going on. Everything going off," she smiled, tucked his covers up under his chin.

Peace, calm, *nuages, nuages, nuages* / clouds, clouds clouds, Debussy's music flowing through her head as she radiated calm across them, Peguy gone, vanished, erased, just night and sleep and *nuages*.

Then out into the living room, just about to switch on the TV, seek out a little news, the latest about the Arabs versus the rest of the world, Israel … what more today … hopefully nothing at all…

When the phone rang.

Alert, wildly reactive, somehow she caught it on the first ring.

"Hello?"

"*C'est moi* / It's me."

Peguy. It couldn't be, but it was.

"Are you crazy?"

"Look out the window. I'm still down here, with my cellular phone."

"How do I know you don't have a rifle or something?"

Him laughing, so loud, in fact, that she could hear him not only on the phone but outside in the street. Peguy times two. A double dose of goofiness.

But getting up, turning off the living room lights, opening the shutters and window, kneeling down with the phone in her hand, looking out. There he still was, Holy Dwarf with Phone.

"You're pure surrealism, Dada."

"I was wondering, how about going for a little icecream? You know that place here on the Île San Luis, just facing Notre Dame."

"They're closed probably. And I have to work tomorrow morning."

"Come on, it's early, you'll have all eternity to rest. And for me … nowadays I see every day as my last day, even enjoy doing it that way, gives things more intensity."

"I'll be down in a few minutes."

"Wonderful!"

Giving her a wave, then both arms up, like he'd just won a tennis match or something. Checking her shoes. Grey suede. Grey suede skirt. Just a bit too short? No. A little lipstick, a quick hair brushing, smiling at her vanity, as if she were going on a date with St. Francis of Assisi or something.

Father Stalker. In the name of the Father, Son and Holy Hunter.

Down on the old lift that should have been replaced fifty years earlier, out the front door, and there he was, bowing Japanese style, hands spread out, flat against each other.

"*Konichiwa!* I'm so glad you decided to come."

"What's this all about?"

"Kind of chilly. I wanted to sit outside."

"Just a little beyond that now."

"Maybe not."

Just a short walk around the corner. And there was the café, the back of Notre Dame, even the back, the buttressed windows, sending a vague thrill of excitement through her. Silly, but there it was, as if The Medieval was flawless, godlike, and the contemporary full of *merde*…

"How did you ever track me down?" she asked as they walked into the café, "and, incidentally, no icecream for me, maybe a little sandwich, a little wine … my treat."

"Don't worry, I'm *loaded*. Years of nothing to spend it on. I almost said 'centuries.' I'm losing it. I guess that's what happens when you're on the edge of eternity."

The waiter, curious at the totally mismatched couple, seating them by the window.

Which was perfect.

Ordering a little sausage sandwich and some *vin rouge*, she didn't care what kind.

But he still insisted on his icecream. And *vin rouge*.

"You introduced yourself when you first came to see me. And I wrote it down, used the phone book. I'm kind of a ferret, I guess, ferret, mole … I burrow into things, never let anything go."

"You're not thinking of anything sexual…?"

"You're kidding. I'm as asexual as you can get. I had prostate cancer some five years ago, they did surgery, cut the nerves, I get Lupron shots every four months. Which makes my ankles swell up, and I have hot flashes, especially at night when I least need them … but in terms of sex … zero … I'm the Kamakura Buddha, the soul, heart, essence of total peace … they ought to try the Lupron shots on those American maniac-priests who seem so interested in little boys, something that I don't even remotely understand. And saying that they were 'gifts from God,' like one of them did. I don't know how the Church can survive in a place like, say Boston…"

"So what *is* your interest all about?"

"I don't know," he said as his icecream appeared, a tiny little mountain topped with rich-looking chocolate that she could smell all the way across the table, a cherry (with stem) on the very top. Her sausage sandwich just as scrumptious. Good place. She'd have to come back, bring her boys with her. "Judaism sometimes seems so much more 'logical' than Catholicism. I mean you go down to Provence, you know, the volcanic areas of France, all the extinct volcanos, boulders … you can't just say they 'happened.' Where do rocks come from? Where does the earth itself come from? And the stars, asteroids, the other planets? Even Aristotle came up with the need for a *first cause, itself uncaused.* God. Turn Him into a father, fine … *baruch ata Adonai Eloheinu melech Ha'olam*…"

"Where did you learn your Hebrew? It's pretty good."

"Curiosity … I like going to Jewish services … have some cassettes I've listened to … things are so much more accessible than they used to be."

"So you want me to convert you to Judaism?"

"No, no, no…" the waiter pouring their wine, Peguy lifting up his glass, toasting, *Lach Heim, Lach Heim* / To Life, To Life, "I'm in the conversion business … but I'm curious about why, what attracted you to Catholicism in the first place?"

"It seems so 'human.' Maybe it's the primitive matriarchal feminist in me, but the Virgin Mother, Christ as a babe in the Virgin's arms … turning all this…" pointing up at the sky beyond the almost-leafless trees, a clear night, the sky full of stars, "turning all this into something 'reachable,' understandable in human terms."

"And what about your sons?"

"Maybe later. The oldest just made his Bar-Mitzvah. No sense complicating their lives too much at this point. Once I'm inside it'll be much easier to come in after me."

"As if the whole thing were a cave."

"It is a cave in a way, protection against the Out There…"

"Although we never really get rid of the sense that we're living inside a mystery, do we? That we don't have a hint as to how the universe began. And how can there be an Uncaused Cause? Everything has to begin, doesn't it? And what was there before the beginning? And how did it begin in the first place?"

"Now you're driving me crazy again," she laughed, her turn to lift up her glass, another Lach Heim. Good wine. She could easily understand how people became and stayed alcoholics, dull it all, deaden it, just turn all the *angst* into one long grey room with the blinds tilted shut.

"Sorry. Any other job and I would have been fired, I guess. A real problem with frankness. You want to start the conversion process … say tomorrow? St. Paul to the Corinthians: 'For the Jews require a sign, and the Greeks seek after wisdom: But we preach Christ crucified, unto the Jews a stumbling block and unto the Greeks foolishness…'"

"There you go again. Christ crucified as a stumbling block to the Jews. I'm not a Cherokee Indian."

"You're not really a 'Jew' either, are you? You're Outer Space-Inner Space right now, aren't you?"

Laughing. More confused than ever. More wine. More and more and more wine. Asking for a second glass. And the sandwich so good, thinking it was probably pork, then dismissing pork as anathema, that made sense when everyone was getting trichinosis and the pig was a sacred animal, but now?

Enjoy, enjoy, enjoy…

Into the now, now, now, and let's just see what comes later.

VI

She came rather gingerly into Peguy's office.

It must have showed.

"Come on in, come on in, I'm not the Big Bad Wolf, and you're certainly not Little Red Riding Hood…"

"Although I do have a red coat on," she laughed, sitting down in this big old wooden chair in front of his desk, him getting up and coming over and sitting in front of her, as if he wanted to eliminate all barriers between them, not make it Preacher and Penitent, but just 'pals.'

"Nice office!" she said, looking around, all kinds of pictures of the Blessed Virgin on the walls, some things very ancient looking, almost medieval, a medievalish statue of Jesus, hand upraised like a Rabbi giving the final blessings after services.

"You like my 'medieval' things? From Holland, actually. After the war. You know. I was there at a conference, Rotterdam, almost totally destroyed … poking around in ruins … they're kind of 'illegal' and all that, but in a sense where better place than this? And how do you like my Mexican Blessed Virgin?"

Pointing to a huge, bright, very 'Indianish' looking picture of the Blessed Virgin.

"A bit garish, but who says Jews aren't garish."

"I've got a little tea here," smiled Peguy getting up and going to a bookcase on which sat what looked like a very, very Louis-the-Fourteenthish teapot and two teacups and a sugar bowl, "just waiting for you. It should be just about right by now…"

Miriam noticing a little sink and microwave over in the far corner of his office half hidden by a carved screen from, she guessed, India.

He was such an artsy guy. She loved it, always had been a frustrated interior designer herself, loved to play around with wallpapers and paints and pictures, mirrors, the perfect chair here, the perfect candlestick there…

"Very 'antiqueish.'"

"I try."

She loaded her tea with sugar and they both sipped a little, then sat back in their chairs, relaxed.

"It's funny, sometimes I play a little game with myself, take a copy of the bible in hand, and just open it randomly," taking a copy of the bible off his desk and opening it randomly, "and invariably it gives me, how shall I put it, 'peace.'" Starting to read: "'Peace I leave with you, my peace I give unto you: not as the world giveth, give I unto you. Let not your heart be troubled, neither let it be afraid...'" stopping, looking a little troubled, confused.

"You had the page marked didn't you?" Miriam teased him, but not just teasing either, it had been too much on the mark to be pure coincidence, hadn't it? Peace, peace, peace...

"No, not really. St. John, Chapter Fourteen, verse 27, and then in Chapter Sixteen, the very end: 'These things I have spoken unto you, that in me ye might have peace. IN the world ye shall have tribulation; but be of good cheer, I have overcome the world.' Hmmmmmm ... I have overcome the world ... how does that strike you. Can't you just feel the peace descend, the Buddha-of-Kamakura-ness?"

"But what about something you said the other day, about the crucifixion being an impediment to the Jewish acceptance of Christ as Messiah?"

"Well, what the Jews *wanted* was someone to liberate them from the Romans. And to see the possible Messiah crucified by the Romans, well, it negated their whole idea of salvation in this world, or maybe *salvation* isn't the right word ... liberation is more like it ... but I think of the sentiment in so many inscriptions in the catacombs, early Christians killed by the Romans, death not as something horrible, this life as something great ... but death as desirable ... suddenly leaving this world behind and going to eternal Heaven to be with God forever."

"But the 'son of God'?"

"Someone had to redeem mankind from Original Sin."

"Original Sin?"

"Adam and Eve, the Garden of Eden, Adam eating the forbidden fruit, which changed the whole nature of man's life on earth, introduced aging, death, disease..."

"But for the son of the God who created the whole universe to have to be scourged and crucified, go through all that agony? It doesn't make any sense to me."

"That's what I originally said, the crucifixion is a big impediment for the Jews to believe in the Christ. I guess I got used to it, was raised in it, the way Christians *concentrate* on Christ's suffering, The Way of the Cross, Christ Falls the First Time, Christ is Crowned with Thorns … but always followed by the Easter Sunday resurrection … Spring, after a long, dead Winter."

"Jesus as sun-god again?"

"Well…" Peguy screwing up his face, "let me put it this way, what we believe influences, dominates, colours and forms our whole lives. If we're Richard Morrises and believe that we're in this endless, godless chance universe that's nothing more than a big question mark, we go around our entire lives under a cloud, strangled by anguish. I know. I've written to Morris, in fact when he came to Paris about ten years ago he stayed with me for a few days, and I never met anyone more – how can I put it, 'resigned.' Like he was going to get hung the following week. I found him extremely defensive, brittle, surrounded by a kind of perpetual howl of, how can I put it, 'desolation.' I mean the Greeks and Hera, Aphrodite, Zeus … all very fanciful, but, for me, at least more science fiction than anything 'real.' And the Jewish lack of any real afterlife … you say Kaddish and all you do is praise God, you have your Jahrzeits, but it's all remembrance, no sense of re-meeting anyone in some sort of woolly-clouded heaven again … whereas Catholicism, it's all spelled out, you see it all over the cathedrals in stone, God the Father, the Son, the Holy Spirit, the Madonna – how/why Madonna ever called herself Madonna I'll never know – and the promise of perpetual beatitude, *per omnia saecula saeculorum, Amen*, if you'll pardon a little Latin."

"*Haolam* in Hebrew, *Olam* is the universe, *Haolam* is 'eternity,'" Miriam getting her two cents in, enjoying more than ever before being who she was, knowing what she knew, like she was the Elder God(ess) talking to some just initiated Young God, *Welcome to the pantheon, I'm one of the old-timers around here*. Felt like getting up, politely, of course, *many thanks* and all that but just leaving…

But didn't. Owed to him, didn't she, to last it out until he finished?

"I know a little Hebrew. A little. After all the services I've attended, you know, but…" getting very solemn suddenly, solemn but at the same time totally defenceless, tears coming into his eyes, looking like a little kid whose cat has just got killed by a car, whose mother has just got killed by terrorists, suddenly thinking of her dead husband, and not just *him* but all the hundreds of Israelis and Palestinians who had been killed over what exactly, where does my backyard end and yours begin? "I'm a Catholic, I stay a Catholic not because I automatically believe, but *choose* to believe, the same way I choose to believe in Renoir and Pissarro and Rachmaninoff and … Paris… *'être dans la nature ainsi qu'un arbre humain /* be in nature like a human tree'."

"You're quoting…?"

"Anna de Noailles … almost unknown … although she shouldn't be. But you see what I mean, I don't want to die and become nothing more than a neanderthalish pile of bones. I don't want to be Jewish and be faced with no real sense of afterlife at all. I want to ascend into Heaven and see the old gang, my fat, old greasy grandmother and slim, stylish mother and the grandfathers I never saw, my grumpy old cigar-smoking father, my dead friends, aunts, uncles … and … will I be able to talk to Jesus and the Blessed Virgin? And what's 'beatitude' like?" lowering his voice as if he didn't want anyone else to hear, as if the Inquisition was outside the door with tape recorders, boss-bishops just waiting for him to reveal all so he could be burned, hung, drawn and quartered in the old inquisitorial style, "I don't know how much I really 'believe-believe,' but I know what I *want* to believe … and what I want to believe, force myself to believe, spreads its light all across the whole of my life, I'm never 'down,' in the dumps, depressed, despairing, but always waiting to ascend into eternal Paradise to be with my hero, my king, my best friend, Jesus … you see what I mean?"

"I see, yes, what you believe 'forms' your whole life. I was just thinking of the Lama."

"The Dalai Lama," he corrected, just a minor, muted footnote.

"The Dalai Lama, how before he died he told everyone 'You want to see how much control I have over my body. You'll see

– no rigor mortis.' And after he died he never got rigor mortis."

"And not just a specific physical effect," Peguy being rather obviously 'patient' with her, "But going to bed at night, lying there in the dark, your most vulnerable moment of the day, just you and … and … that's the point…WHAT? Don't you hate the idea of being in a universe where WHAT is NOTHING … CHANCE? But imagine, in the ancient past, the idea of the Great Mother, the Earth was literally Mother Earth, you slept in the arms, in the womb, whatever, of the Great Mother. Sometimes I wish I could go all the way back to that…"

"But the Virgin Mary is almost the same. All the cathedrals. Notre Dame. Our Lady…"

"True enough. But, please … no 'automatic' universes … sleep in the arms of Our Lady, fine … talking to her son, Jesus… 'Help me, Jesus, get through the night,' all my prostate problems and swollen legs and joints caused by the chemotherapy…" stopping, looking very, very old, ancient, Miriam for a moment thinking of the ancient French, Mouster, Mousterian paleolithic spearpoints, skulls, how we'd all end up as interesting skulls, and then, when/if the skulls decayed, as nothing at all, Peguy reaching over and picking up his bible, "Let God guide me, in fact, open a page at random, which isn't random at all, but very much 'guided,'" opening it up, "John 12 … let's see what we have here. Thirty years ago I could have practically recited it for you, but not any more. Jesus glorified by the Jews, 'They took branches of palm trees, and went forth to meet him, and cried 'Hosanna, blessed is the King of Israel that cometh in the name of the Lord.' The origin of Palm Sunday. You see how closely the primitive Church stayed to the text. And look here, verse 24, 'Except a grain of wheat fall into the ground and die, it abideth alone, but if it die it bringeth forth much fruit … he that loveth his life shall lose it, and he that hateth his life in this world shall keep it unto life eternal.' An explanation of sorts for the Death and Resurrection. Jesus becomes a seed that has to die in order to bring forth life. Then there's this whole thing about 'walking in the light.' All this business about the Father having sent Him… 'I am come as a light into the world, and whoever believeth in me should not abide in darkness.' Just what I was saying before … there I am in the darkness of my bed, I'm a terrible sleeper, rely on all sorts of herbs to knock me out, and still I don't sleep … but it's OK, in my darkness, close to death, my whole body saying one thing 'Not much longer now,' but it's OK because in the midst of my physical darkness, I'm surrounded by The Trinity, God the Father, huge and bearded and all benevolence, the father I never had, the Holy Spirit dove asleep on its perch at the far end of the room, Jesus, sitting there in the darkness sipping on a glass of dark, sweet kosher wine, *Lach Heim, Lach Heim, Lach Heim* / To Life, To Life, To Life. And over the whole house the Blessed Virgin wearing her blue and white cape, breathing softly blessing, blessing blessing everything around her. It's sanity. It's better than Haldol and psychiatry, to turn the universe around you into *Shantih, Shantih, Shantih,* the peace that passeth understanding…"

Sitting back in his chair, beyond age now, dead and already passed over into eternity, Miriam finding it very easy to imagine him up in a blessed cloudworld somewhere for all eternity, much the same as he was right now.

For some long moments just basking in Peguy's peace that passeth understanding, and then reaching over and lifting up the bible herself.

"Let me play your game for a moment, OK?"

"What game is that?"

"Turning randomness into divine revelation."

"If that's the way you see it…"

A little hurt, obviously not wanting her, her cynicism dominating at all for the moment, not wanting to come back into 'reality' at all … ever…

She opened the bible.

Psalm 93. Started to read:

"The Lord reigns, he is clothed with majesty, The Lord is clothed with strength, with which He has clothed himself. The world is established so that it cannot be moved. Thy throne is established of old and Thou art from Everlastingness…"

Peguy snapping back into peace again.

"Sounds pretty good to me. Everlasting strength, majesty … peace … all the Catholics have done is 'explicate' the oneness and seen it divided into three parts … but the unity, the oneness is still there … and a little bit of the Magna Mater/ Great Mother/Blessed Virgin never hurt anyone."

Smiling.

Trivializing it all in a way, but that was OK too. Somehow its peace dripping off on her, like drops of rain from trees as you walk through a misty forest. Feeling Him there as never before, Him in all His three aspects, and the whole room enclosed in the mantle of the Great Mother Virgin (why Virgin?) beyond questioning into the world of total acceptance.

A few months of their little 'games,' and by Winter she was ready for Baptism.

On the altar at Notre Dame.

"But what's it all about?" asked Adam as she got dressed for the Baptism.

"Like a Mikvah, I guess … some sort of ritual cleansing … washing away of sins, bringing you into the fold."

"Fold?"

"*Nous sommes toutes moutons, n'est ce pas?* / We're all sheep, aren't we? Jesus is the Lamb of God."

"Why not the pig?" quipped Michael.

"It's all Jewish," she said, all in white today, her first time ever all in white, skirt maybe a bit too short, heels maybe a bit too high, white stockinged legs a bit too shapely, "but … like the Mass, Communion, it's all based on Passover, the bread and wine, and the lamb, the lamb of God, Baptism. It's all Jewish … just 'updated,' hating the word when it came out, 'updated,' part of her still wanting to be un-updated, ancient, primal, like Rabbi Frankel was always saying "The best religions are the earliest religions, the further back the more sense it makes … even turning everything into gods … the divine."

But still wanting to be 'in,' part of the 'fold.'

"But am I still going to do my Bar-Mitzvah?" asked Adam.

"Of course, of course. Later on, if you decide to follow your mother across the Sea of Reeds…"

"Sea of Reeds?"

"Red Sea … that's a more accurate translation."

A sudden image of ancient Egyptians pursuing ancient Jews filling her mind, the Jews crossing over as the Egyptians pursued them, and then the water suddenly giving way, coming back together, killing them all. Lazarus rising from the dead, Jesus rising from the dead, the empty tomb on Easter (Passover) Sunday … wanting to believe that the Messiah had actually come, The Omnipotent on two legs with long hair, speaking Aramaic, the Hebrew of Christ's time, still used in the Kaddish … and that some day (soon?) He would come back and the world would end in cloudy, heavenly glory.

"I don't want to go. Do we have to go?" asked Michael. "It's kind of a scary place … all those columns and stone and what if a terrorist bombs it or something…"

"Don't be ridiculous, a terrorist bomb Notre Dame? Whatever for?"

"What did they ever bomb our father for, he didn't do anything."

A horrible sense of loss suddenly filling her, like a bucket of black tar had been poured all over her, a bucket of shit, swamp water … what next, East Nile virus, a mosquito in the Bois du Boulogne?

"You're both going, and that's it!" she said, *never* a dictatorial mother, always sweet and gingerish, Ms. ginger candle, dispersing her perfume into the air of everyone around her. Although … sometimes you had to be Franco, Allende, William the Conqueror, didn't you…?

"OK," they both said, practically together, back into their bedroom, their computer, the new Mario games. It was nice to have that big bankroll in the old bank, wasn't it? Sometimes worried about a depression, the bottom falling out of the French economy, felt she should have her money in Switzerland, but now with Switzerland becoming part of the rest of the European community, losing its 'isolation' in a way.

Ça suffit, ça suffit … let it go, let it go…

A nice hot shower, and then the blessing of bed. Loving Paris for a moment, for a moment looking out the window at the Seine and all the apartment buildings on the other side of the river, half moon just rising, and loving it all, the revolutions and Bastille days and the student riots and black Africans and North African Arabs, the impressionists and Hemingway and Henry Miller, Rodin, the Rodin Museum, the officiousness of M. Eiffel and his monster tower, the budding trees, *plus de temps, plus de temps, plus de temps* … more time, more time, more time …horribly guilty for a moment as she thought how lucky (God-gifted?) she had been not to have gone to that pizza parlour where her husband had been killed. Clothes off. Making the shower hotter than usual, Patchouli soap, loving her breasts and legs and hairy pubic triangle for a moment, just to be there in the glorious NOW, then, as she stepped into the hot water, calming down, *In Nomine Patris, Filii et Spiritus Sancti … Father, Son and Holy Spirit…*

Then suddenly her mind starting to sing in Hebrew: shalom aleichem, malachei ha-shar-reit, malachei Elyon … Peace unto you O ministering angels, messengers of the Most High…

Peace.

Paix.

The angels in the shower with her, all wet wings and blessedness, welcoming them all, like being in a box of chickens, smiling, then laughing, welcome, welcome, welcome … all the angels but the Angel of Death. She never wanted to see him again, for many, many years, loving the idea now that she'd been such a 'Jewish mother' to her kids. Good for them. Keep them on track in a trackless world.

The next afternoon in Notre Dame, up the main aisle up to the nave, under the curved stone ceilings that looked like stone crabs, past all the stained glass windows, everything curved, rosetted, vast, almost sepulchral, Father Peguy up on the main altar waiting for her like the little castrated/prostate-surgeried elf that he was, smiling, a triumph for him, no?

"I'm scared!" said Michael, "I like synagogues, but this –"

"Science-fictionish, no?"

"Yes!"

"You'll be fine," Miriam suddenly getting soft and motherly like she'd never been before, "it's been here for a thousand years, and it'll be here for another thousand, at least…"

"A thousand years?" Adam the mathematician, her little computer nerd, his head boiling with the number 1,000 …

although what was a mere thousand for her, her Semitic ancestors, her 'tribe', going back, back, back to God knows where/when.

"It won't take long," bending down and kissing them both on their heads. Nicely clean heads. She made sure of that. Just a touch of Patchouli, the only shampoo she ever bought, a little touch of Hindu sensuality, just what they needed, both of them so totally in their heads, in their computers, internet, computer-games, the whole electronic business creating a whole new generation of nerdified pure heads, no bodies, senses…

Smiling as she went up the rest of the altar to her mentor, Mad Father Peguy, whom she loved, loved, loved for his frankness, honesty, even his confusion.

So small and tiny up there on the altar dwarfed by the mausoleumish magnificence of the cathedral itself.

Were they believers or not, the original builders? Like all 'founders', 'beginners', always the first buildings of any city the best, whether it be London, Jerusalem or … thinking Nineveh … Kabul…

Too much history. Too much reading.

NOW, NOW, NOW … forcing herself back into her body, her white nylon-sleek legs, her almost little-girlish white-made-up face that hid all the wrinkles – almost – up to the main altar.

"*Bonjour, mon amie. Tous va bien?* / Hello, my friend. Everything OK?"

"*Magnifique!*"

Some tourists coming into the church, Germans, she thought, wasn't that German she was hearing as they oohed and aahed about the size and magnificence of the place, remembering her visit to Cologne (Köln) the year before. They had their own magnificent cathedrals, *nicht wahr?* They should have stuck with them … how did the Führer ever emerge from the country of Beethoven, Bach, Schumann, Brahms?

"Just ignore them, they'll behave themselves," smiled Peguy, nodding toward the tourists. "I've got so used to them that they're practically invisible … and inaudible. I see you brought your boys along. Will they be next?"

"I don't know." Miriam not appreciating the question at all.

"When they're old enough to decide. I don't want to disrupt them psychologically too much, there's been enough discontinuity in their lives already … how about a few years of simple continuity?"

"Continuity, discontinuity, your French is getting … it must be very difficult with all the roots so different."

"It's not easy although I took French in college … a little bearded professor from the Sorbonne, in fact."

"Wonderful." Then moving suddenly from Father Benign Old Saint to Father Business-at-Hand, "You kneel here … it may be a bit messy for you, but holy water it is and holy water it has to be…"

Handing her a little container to catch the water in, starting to pray in Latin, her smiling as she remembered him going on one day about Vatican II ("all the Vaticans") and the getting rid of Latin ("in order to de-universalize the universal church") and him insisting that he was too old to change, and besides he loved Latin … beginning to pray … in Latin … the tourists coming up to the front of the church, kneeling down and watching, suddenly becoming piously quiet, a few words passing between them, probably, she thought, about her being an adult, an adult being baptized, did she look Semitic enough for them to be able to tell, tempted for a moment to stand up and call out MA HADASH to them – WHAT'S NEW?

But behaving herself as Peguy got to the centre of the ritual *Ego te baptizo in nomine Patris, et Filii, et Spiritus Sancti* / I baptize thee in the Name of the Father, the Son and the Holy Spirit. Not much water. And he had a big towel that he handed her to help her wipe off her forehead, as she got through drying herself off noticing Michael and Adam in the back of the church getting up and getting out fast, although with a certain amount of dignity, deference to the sense of the place being 'sacred,' even if scary.

The German tourists out there all happy as they finished up, smiling, applauding without really clapping their hands, totally noiselessly, all that blond hair and bulk, one man especially looking like he'd just come out of some neanderthal museum somewhere, remembering how the name 'neanderthal' came from a place called the Valley of Neander … feeling truly 'cleansed,' 'at peace,' reaching over and giving Father Peguy a little kiss on the cheek. Which scandalized-amused the Germans.

Then following some wild impulse in herself, the altar becoming *bima*, suddenly becoming a rabbi, rabbinically in charge, *the older the better*, isn't that what Peguy always said during his ramblings? Going up to the tabernacle, knowing the Torah wasn't there, no scrolls, no Hebrew, but opening it up and making the sign of the cross, there was the empty chalice, intoning in Hebrew, just barely above a whisper: "*Baruch ata Adonai Eloheinu Melech ha'olam borei pri hagafen* / Holy Art Thou, God, God, King of the Universe, Creator of the Fruit of the Wine.

The Germans all confused, scandalized again but this time not simultaneously amused, wanting to turn around and say something to them in her grandmother's Lithuanian Yiddish, but controlling herself … coming back to Father Peguy, who, surprisingly, had tears in his eyes, looking like some old grandma himself, giving her an embrace.

"I know it's crazy, but I loved it, the blessing of the wine."

"How do you know that?" she smiled, always amazed by the man, what he knew that he really shouldn't know.

"Oh, I don't know … for someone as close to Kaddish as me … I've always been curious, actually learned how to read Hebrew at one point, love the sound of *Melech Ha'olam*, King of the Universe … it's like a taste for dark chocolate or chirimoya icecream."

"Chirimoya?"

"Bolivia. The most heavenly fruit you'll ever taste."

Another little hug.

"If you weren't a hundred and ten and a priest, I swear…"

Him laughing.

"Me too," moving down off the altar now, "come over to my office, there are some papers to sign, after we find your boys."

"So you noticed too. The church overwhelmed them."

"It overwhelms me too." Passing by the Germans, waving to them, hand out, which they grabbed and shook, "*Guten tag, guten tag, guten tag…*" as he passed beyond them toward the back of the church kind of letting his mind wander, letting his thoughts just come out, "There never was a second world war, Puten, whatever his name is, is Mr Big Business, everything absolved, forgotten, Hitler never was, the Gestapo, Auschwitz and Belsen … *l'histoire, l'histoire, l'histoire…*"

As Miriam emerged out into the cold sun feeling somehow ashamed, cowardly, the kind of sneaky bitch she never wanted to be, no mention of any of this to anyone at the Temple, big hidden secret, she had to protect her job didn't she, even if she didn't need the money, had to protect *what?* Just wanting to keep it all under cover, two hers, Jekyll and Hyde, only which was which?

Cold sun.

L'hiver de nos jours / The winter of our days.

Suddenly feeling she was as old as Peguy and then some, it had all gone, was going so fast, her head filled with her dead father and mother and her cousins who had been killed on a school bus in Tel Aviv, her dead grandmothers and grandfathers, Abraham and Sarah and Pharaoh … and Jesus Himself.

Looking up at the sky as if she expected Him to be coming back (again?) riding on a white (horse) cloud.

"*Temps pour le jugement final.* / Time for the final judgement."

"It wouldn't be a bad time for it, would it?" smiled Peguy as Michael and Adam came from around the back of the cathedral, Michael all enthusiastic, "Man, you've gotta see the back of this place, all the stained glass windows and stone supports…"

"The apse and the buttresses," smiled Peguy.

"Whatever you say," Michael put down, feeling stupid.

Which wasn't Peguy's intention at all, Miriam knew that, but…

"Would you be surprised if he became an architect?"

"Not at all, not at all … that's how it all begins, *should* begin, some focusing in, fun … and then you *become* your interests."

Stopping at the bottom of the steps, a moment of unexpected sadness for Miriam. She didn't want to leave Peguy. What did she want? For all four of them to go home to some home in the almost-country (somewhere along the Loire?) Mansard roofs and a big living room with a chandelier in it, big, light bedrooms, a garden with a gazebo in it, comfort, comfort, comfort, just being, *être, être, être* / to be, to be, to be, with comfortable, zany old Peguy, watching the boys grow up under his/their influence, to be, to be, to be … until they simply weren't … and then, were there really cloudy heavens up there somewhere where they'd all be reunited forever and forever and forever?

Wanting there to be.

In the name of the Father, the Son and the Holy Spirit. And what she wanted *happened*, didn't it, became reality for her. Almost.

VII

When she woke up in the hospital, all covered with bandages, she didn't really need anyone to tell her what had happened. She was getting to be like an expert in all the worst kinds of twisted, perverted madnesses.

The nurse taking the temperature of an old woman in the bed next to her, noticing her waking up.

"I don't know … a moment … I'll…"

Hurriedly leaving the ward, the old lady next to her complaining, "What about me?" the thermometer still in her mouth, Miriam worried about her biting it, you could kill yourself off with a piece of thermometer glass, couldn't you?

"Don't talk!" said Miriam sternly, surprising the old woman who obviously wasn't used to being treated like an erring child.

"Excuse me!"

But she stopped talking, as the nurse returned with a doctor, a little man who looked very Arab, probably wasn't, but…

"Bonjour. I'm Doctor Martinu. How's it going?"

"You tell me."

"Nothing broken. Some rather deep wounds from flying glass, but I sewed them all up, no big problem. Just lucky you didn't get any glass in your eyes, you could have ended up blind. Or that no big arteries were severed, you could have ended up bleeding to death by the time they had got to you. What a horrible time of the year to do such things, and colder than usual. A lot of pneumonias out of all this, I'm sure…"

"As if there would ever have been a 'right' time of year? As if summer would have been OK?"

"That's not what I meant, I…"

All ready to turn around and leave.

Such a bland-looking little guy, almost a midget. Looked so 'dark.' Wondering about the French for a moment, the movements of peoples out of ancient Anatolia and India into Europe, constant nomadism, skulls, the amazing tenacity of genes being passed down over thousands and thousands of years, 'nordics' versus 'the south people,' was there any purpose, design, "why" in any of it, was it all just chance, chance, chance?

"What about my boys?" she asked, suddenly forgetting herself, her pain, her almost-death altogether, totally involved with them, them, them.

"Your boys?"

"My two sons in the back of the church. I was up receiving communion, and they were in the back…"

Not knowing what to say, his face all torture and agony.

"Two boys in the back alone?"

Checking the papers on the clip-board he had in his right hand.

"Not all the bodies have been identified yet, but…"

"The bodies?"

"The explosion was at the back of the church, the main body of the church, to get the maximum number of people I suppose, the main altar itself … it's such a ruin … a thousand years, I don't know, I never was very good at history, but…"

"What do you mean the bodies?"

"You'll have to identify them, of course, but…"

"They weren't killed…?"

"I'm afraid…" tears in the little man's eyes, totally defeated now, you get to the point when you think that all the revolutions and terrors are over, that you've finally made it to a vast ocean of infinite peace, and … wasn't anyplace, anyplace, anyplace safe, secure? "You wouldn't feel up to identifying the bodies right now, would you? We'd kind of like to get things –"

"Buried? Is that the word?"

"*Plus tard, plus tard* / later, later," and he started to walk away, like erasing a blackboard, tearing up a sheet of paper, instant amnesia.

"No, now! Now!"

Throwing back her covers, starting to get out of the bed, damn the consequences, crazy, knowing she was crazy wanting to be crazy, that was what the moment demanded, wasn't it?

"No, no, no … take it easy, let me get you a wheelchair, you can't be walking about in your condition."

Lying back down, waiting while he went and came back with a wheelchair, thinking that maybe the boys hadn't got

75

killed, there was always the possibility that they'd already gone out the way they usually did at Notre Dame, that they were outside, safe and sound somewhere, looking for her ... but not really believing that ... Psalm 19 suddenly there in her mind, "My soul cleaveth unto the dust..."

Dust we are and to dust we shall return.

The doctor back now. With a fat-faced nurse, her face all screwed up into a scowl permanently, maybe some sort of accident, a stroke ... or maybe she was just born that way. Blonde with black-grey roots.

"Here, let's get you into this."

No real 'deep' pain, just surface ... skin ... lots of that ... lucky that she'd escaped with her two eyes intact, would have hated to have been blind, attached as she was to the aesthetics of seeing, every sunset or full or half moon or no moon at all, just the streets, street-lights, shopfronts, the Seine, old buildings, a Sumerian at heart, when she was a kid always wanting to inhabit ancient ruins in the middle of the nowhere desert, pull old stones in around her and forget the modern world altogether.

Into the wheelchair, down the corridor into the lift, down to the basement, the doctor's face getting more and more agitated, worried, concerned, Miriam thinking *he knows already, doesn't he, il sait tout, he knows everything* ... wondering how they could be so crazy to be taking her down into this Frankensteinish-Draculaish morgue when she was as wounded as she was, how about some sedatives, knock her out, protect from the reality she was being wheeled into.

"Here we are..."

A young guy in a long white coat, tragic-faced, pulling out two 'trays' with bodies on them.

Michael and Adam.

Of course.

It was as inevitable as pollen and hay fever, a cold shower and shivering.

Their little faces all bloodied up, bodies broken, what happened to all the doctors and lawyers and writers and wives and grandchildren now, what was left for her, aloneness, aloneness, aloneness, one of the psalms suddenly coming into her head … *Esa Enai el heharim* … I lift up my eyes to the mountains: what is the source of my help? Lord, Maker of heaven and earth, he will not allow your foot to slip … the sun shall not harm you by day, nor the moon by night … the Lord will guard you from all evil.

"*Merde!* Shit!"

Suddenly everything she had ever, ever believed gone, there was nothing Out There but pain, madness, chance. If God had created man why hadn't He created him sane, good, balanced … the French against the Arabs and now the Arabs reacting … action-reaction, endless pain, as if the volcanos and floods and hurricanes and half the world frozen half of every year weren't enough.

"*Ça suffit, je ne peut pas plus* / Enough, I can't take any more."

Getting up out of her wheelchair and going over and hugging her boys, wishing she had the touch of God herself, bring them back to life, *and the third day He rose from the dead* … so rise, rise, rise, my babies, my life, her dead husband's genes now gone forever, always feeling that they were part of him, as long as they were alive, part of him still alive, now all of it gone, gone, gone.

The doctor all disturbed.

"With all your stitches, you really should…"

Nodding toward the morgue attendant in his white coat, trying to get her back into the wheelchair, but no go.

"DON'T TOUCH ME!"

Out of the morgue as fast as she could stumble along, pulling her bandages off as she went, everyone trying to catch up with her, hold her, stop her, starting to scream now.

"KEEP AWAY FROM ME, I'M NOT A PRISONER, I'VE DONE NOTHING WRONG, JUST EVERYTHING RIGHT, YOU HAVE NO RIGHT TO STOP ME, HOLD ME, HURT ME ANY MORE…"

Getting into the lift, just ahead of them as they hesitated, the doctor pulling out a little wireless phone, dialling, she knew, for security, bring the cops in, stop her at any cost.

But she wouldn't be stopped, they were Egyptians, the doctor was Pharaoh, Egyptians, Philistines, Nazis, terrorists, whatever.

First floor. Out the revolving door.

"Taxi!"

And the taxi, faster than she'd ever seen a taxi respond to a call before, immediately there, into the back seat.

"Île San Luis!"

No money, no key … but she'd break down the door, get the money out of the sock at the back of the bottom drawer of her dresser, get to an ATM, more money, money, money … escape to … get away from…

Or maybe it was better to just end it now, like, who was it, the Emperor Tiberius Caesar, just get into the bathtub and cut her wrists, get a little drunk first, a bottle of nice sweet kosher wine, and *then* the bathtub, one of those super-sharp kitchen knives she'd bought the year before, that cut through steel, just cut her wrists a little, let the blood drip out, maybe take a bunch of tylenols with the wine, she'd hardly notice the pain then, end it all, no hope, no future, just thousands of years of past, all buried now, her whole personal landscape just graves and bones and skulls now, what kind of a God-Devil was up there in the sky to create us to live, what, sixty, seventy, eighty, ninety years, when sea-turtles lived for hundreds of years, and then fill the universe with insane terrorists, murderers, rapists, soldiers, nations, Austro-Hungarian empires, Nazi empires, or the tribes in Afghanistan, Tribe Booba-Bobba against Tribe Boola-Boola, different languages, different skin-colours, noses, religions … all out in the Desert of Nothingness growing poppies for opium … killing each other…

Directing the driver to her apartment, such a shit-place, she should have moved out into the country somewhere, down to the Loire Valley, taken her (her husband's) money and bought a decent house and just enjoyed the river, the river, the river…

"I'll be right back with the money, I have to go upstairs and get it, I left the hospital without anything … but my wounds."

The driver smiling.

It was funny, wasn't it?

Ringing Monsieur Beaudry's bell, the old man who lived next door to her. Widower. Former maths teacher. Never, never, never went out, except to shop … lived on sausages, which theoretically should have killed him off years earlier

78

(now 91), but which he seemed to thrive on. Sausages and vin rouge. Answering the bell.

"*Qui est la?* / Who's there?"

"*Moi, Miriam.*"

"But what about your own key?"

"I lost it."

"OK."

The buzzer ringing and her pushing the door open, most of the bandages off now, in the cab, looking at the sewed-up cuts on her arms and legs as she rode up in the lift to her floor, Monsieur Beaudry standing in his doorway when she got there.

"What happened to you?"

"Notre Dame. The terrorists. Haven't you heard?"

"Heard? I heard it all right, thought this whole building would come down too. That's all that's been on the television all day … damned Arabs…"

"Not damned Arabs, damned terrorists! There's a difference."

"And your boys?"

Couldn't answer. Started banging her shoulder against the door, trying to break it down, Beaudry running out as best as he could, hunchbacked little toad that he was, stopping her banging into the door.

"I have a key, no need to break it down!"

"You have a key? Since when?"

"Centuries," he smiled. Mr Wrinkles, but a round, white plate of a face that said "Friends, life is good, the sun shall return, spring is never that far away." And he went in and got a key, handed it to her, "It's yours now."

"It was always mine," she said nastily.

"But if I hadn't had it … see … see…"

"*Merci, mon ami,*" bending over and giving him a kiss, for a mad moment thinking *what if we were married, the two of us, me and this old 'saint,' the rest of our days together, not too bad* … then dismissing the idea as total madness.

Going into the apartment, full of books and TV games, shoes, robes, all the boys' things, full of fury against The Sky/God/The Gods again, back into her bedroom, getting the money out of a red sock in the bottom drawer of her dresser, getting big thick scissors out of the top drawer, cutting off the rest of her bandages, then going into the bathroom and putting band-aids on the wounds, getting out a bunch of long-sleeved shirts and long skirts, tights, a pair of heavy, clumpy black suede shoes, sticking them in the bag, a just-in-case duplicate key to her car in a blue sock in the bottom drawer of her dresser, *fuck it all, all, all,* two little pictures of her dead husband and now dead boys, into this big, ugly (the uglier the better) bag, downstairs, the cabbie waiting…

"I'm going to have to charge you for my waiting-time too."

Wanted to tell him "Charge this!" and give him the finger, but instead forcing herself to be calm, 'nice', *joli, joli, joli,* hearing Debussy's Maid with the Flaxen Hair in her head, thinking *I should have spent my whole life in concerts, studied piano … or drums … imagine being a drummer for Tchaikovsky's Fourth, cymbalist, drummer,* imagining herself for a moment on the top of some huge mountain somewhere, back in Israel, Mount Sinai … a control panel of some kind in front of her, pushing the big red button in the middle, the world-destroyer, what difference would it make, all the little 'worlds' in infinite space, like pebbles on an infinite beach, nobody there to care, if anywhere *was* there, He would have come back and settled not just the Israeli-Palestinian problem, but what about Pakistan and India and Afghanistan, all the tribes, tribes, tribes…

"*Pas problème* / no problem" she said, paying him what he asked for, "*j'ai perdu mon mari et deux infants* / I've lost my husband and two children," tears uncontrollably rolling down her cheeks now, "I have to go and get my car … across the river … *pas loin* / not far."

Hearing her French, her brutal, brusque accent, like chopped garlic, like paleolithic spear points, Mouster, Mousterian … wishing she could time-travel back to the sixty thousand, a hundred thousand B.C.E., Before the Common Era, instead of B.C., Before Christ, another Jewish way of sidestepping The Saviour.

Getting in the cab, pulling in her bag after her, letting it sprawl across the seat, Saviour? God the Father, Son and Holy Spirit …Where were they now, now, now?

Across the river, more time-travelling now, the Left Bank, the Latin Quarter, there were Satie, Debussy, Hemingway, Anaïs Nin … all the paintings of Renoir of nineteenth century beer-gardens she would have liked to have walked into and sat down and had a beer and waited for someone to "May I join you?" answering "Of course!" starting all over again and again and again … eternal reincarnations.

Paris after the revolutions were all ancient history, before World War I and the horrors of World War II … that period of cute hats and bright eyes, little girls and boys, beer-gardens and *l'impressionisme* when all they wanted to do, Monet, Pissarro, Sisley, Degas … the whole army of them … when all they wanted to do was to capture, capture, capture the snows and the trees and the faces, the streets, beauty, beauty, beauty everywhere, not like now when everything was like a huge boulder hung over the top of the world by a thick rope that was slowly snapping and cracking into pieces.

"Just across the river, to the right."

"OK."

Across the Seine, Notre Dame behind her to her left, what was left of it, centuries of beauty and now The Madness had spread everywhere.

Killing Catholics in Pakistan Catholic churches … tourists in Balinese night-clubs. For a moment imagining royal barges coming down the river centuries back. Sanity in a way, *n'est ce pas*, the royal family and all the nobles and the peasants.

Loving the old bridges.

Pont Neuf. How new? Three or four centuries? So many tramps around these days, The Third World … you have colonies and you pay the price … although part of her loved *les Africains et les Arabs* … and so many of them making it 'in,' inside the society, up there, up on top, the new royalty.

Turning right across the bridge, two blocks.

"Right here."

Stopping, getting out, reaching into her pocket to get money to pay him.

"Forget it," starting to drive away, then stopping, "Listen … take it easy … you look – forget it, take it easy."

Kissing his hand and then blowing the kiss her way.

Strangely effeminate, she thought, but she liked it just because it was so spontaneously unexpected, blew him a kiss too, then into the garage, the attendant looking at her, smiling, but not sure how to react. Did she look *that* bad?

One glance over her shoulder back across the river, Notre Dame, still smouldering. What was there to burn? All stone, maybe the bombs themselves still smouldering, helicopters overhead, police everywhere, the history of Paris suddenly there in front of her, the revolutions and counter-revolutions, guillotines and bastilles, over and over again, you'd think it would be time to take Paris off the rack and give it a break, let it flower and sing and soar.

"Bonjour."

"Bonjour, Madame."

"Bonne journée / have a good day."

Down to the lower level where she kept her car.

You didn't know what was coming next, did you? It was going to be like Israel now, wasn't it, you never knew what bus or pizza parlour or museum might be blown up, thinking for a moment of the glass pyramid they'd built in the courtyard of the Louvre, not that it 'fits,' some kind of wild attempt to splice the super-modern with the Rococo...

Taking the lift to the lower level, getting into her little Suburu. Petrol almost on Full. Bom! Bom!

Out onto the streets, through police check-points, everything held up, stopped, having to show her driver's licence over and over again, although apart from the police, the streets looked normal enough, the bakeries and the street-vendors, the legs and the heels, the fat, anxious old men and the little kids, school dismissed probably, until they got the gestapo back in place, that's what it was going to be like, wasn't it...

Not knowing where she was going, just out, out, away, to the south somewhere, out of Paris, the faces of Michael and Adam still pursuing her, their voices, *je suis fatigué, Mama* / I'm tired, *j'ai soif* / I'm thirsty, *je ne peut pas étudier plus* / I can't study any more, then a thousand *je t'aimes* / I-love-yous circling around her head, feeling their arms embrace her as if they were there, hearing her dead husband's voice talking to her, Mr Careful, a lot of good it did him, Mr Cautious, the soul

82

of prudence ... and fear... *Don't do anything crazy now, you've still got yourself, you've still got, what, forty more years...*

"Forty more years of what?" screaming at the empty air.

Slowly making her way out of Paris, which she felt she'd never see again, Sacré Coeur, the Seine, south, south, south, Choisy-le-Roi, Villeneuve, St. Georges, Melun, Montereau, feeling her heart calm down a bit as she moved out into the now-barren countryside some snow on the ground, although it had been mild most of the winter, no idea where she was going, wild at first, expecting to get picked up by the police, but no one touched her, the roads unexpectedly empty as she got further and further out of town, wanting to die in a way, wanting there to be a patch of ice she'd slip on, or a cliff she could drive over to her death, nothing making any sense at all ... only ... as the landscape turned more and more into farms, little ancient villages that hardly seemed touched by the last five centuries at all, simple-arse types along the road, wanting it to be summer, wanting to be back here in summer immersed in leaves and the flowers she knew had to be coming back.

Suddenly tired, 'human' again, not just an insane gargoyle, but an (almost) middle-aged woman all cut-up and bruised, wanting to find a little place to settle down for the night, as the sun began to hit the horizon, castles here and there on the tops of hills, little villages down below the castles, all spelling out the structures of medieval times, the Lords and Ladies and the peasants ... *peut-être* better that way, keep it all in line, under control, amazed at this one huge rock formation on top of a hill, lightly-snow-covered vineyards at the bottom, thinking 'paleolithic,' never forgetting how it all, Israel, here in France, how it *all* had so much prehistory, ancient, ancient peoples doing their thing(s) here, there, everywhere, always the sex-impulse overriding everything else, produce, produce, produce, reproduce, reproduce, reproduce, if it *wasn't* there, the human race would never have survived at all, all the black nyloned legs and tits and arse and...

Past a beautiful château...

Into the village itself.

Stopping and asking an old man in workclothes, heavy coat on, walking leaning on a bike.

"*Comment s'appelle cette ville?* What's the name of this town?"

"*Il n'est pas le meilleur moment pour le tourisme!* / It's not the best time for tourism!"

A smile creasing his worn-out face that to her for a moment looked very Israeli, very Jewish. Who knew what paleolithic backgrounds went into the makings of that face, how long he and his ancestors had been there, there, there and nowhere else. 20,000 years. Was it possible that anyone, any family could have lived there for twenty thousand years?

"*Mais le nom?* / But the name?"

"Avallon."

"*Merci.*"

And she drove into the heart of the village, found a spot on a side street where she could park her car, and got out, keeping repeating the name of the place, *Avallon, Avallon*, remembering something about Lamartine being born around here somewhere, all the endless reading she'd done when she was learning French.

Feeling she was back, back, back in the fifteenth century as she walked the streets, finding a *boulangerie*, going in, some tables in the back.

"*C'est aussi un restaurant ici?* / Is it also a restaurant here?"

"Dans l'hiver non, mais…/*In the winter no, but…*"

And the old, white-haired woman behind the counter, surrounded by piles of bread that smelled utterly delicious, came out and brought her back to a table.

"*Peut-être un sandwich de quelque-chose…* / Maybe a sandwich of something…"

The woman winking, another creased, ancient-faced smile, like the guy with the bike, Miriam wishing she could just 'pass,' didn't have such a monstrously obvious accent, the old lady going back into what was obviously a kitchen, five minutes later coming out with a chicken breast sandwich on a hard-crusted, soft-as-cloud-inside roll.

"*Un peu de vin?*"

"*Rouge?*"

Another smile, and out she came with a big full glass of red wine, some inerasable instinct inside Miriam blessing the wine, *Baruch ata Adonai Eloheinu Melech ha'olam borei pri hagafen* /

Holy are you God, God, King of the Universe, Creator of the Fruit of the Vine."

Tears filling her eyes as she bit into the glorious hard crust, into the bread and then the chicken, a slice of tomato, some watercress, a slice of onion, a thin slice of Roquefort cheese, as if she'd never had a sandwich before in her life, *Qadosh, Qadosh, Qadosh* / Holy, Holy, Holy, and for a moment believing it all, that God was in charge of the world, lifting up the sun in the morning and carrying it down at night, sweeping the clouds across the skies, bringing the rain, bringing the snow, everything in His hands, *Baruch ata Adonai Eloheinu Melech ha'olam*, Holy art Thou, God, God, King of the Universe.

Then suddenly seeing the faces of her dead sons and dead husband again.

Shit, that's all it was, something that just 'happened,' no one out there guiding anything, all the trees and flowers, clouds, volcanos, all of it just chance, chance, chance. She'd have to read the works of Richard Morris some time, that guy who Father Peguy was always talking about, wondering about Peguy himself now, he'd been the one celebrating Mass when the bombs had exploded. Sweet old guy, seeing him at the same time as friend, lover, father, holy man guide…

Finishing up her sandwich, the gusto gone, but finishing it up anyhow, along with her wine, and then suddenly feeling a thousand years old, like she could sleep the rest of her life away.

Paying, and then asking the bakery woman, "I need a place to stay the night, you wouldn't happen to…"

"It's hardly the time for tourism," she smiled. "I feel sorry for you, you seem…"

"Wounded?"

"Yes, wounded, *blessée*."

"I was in Notre Dame when it was blown up."

"Oh, my God, how horrible. It's such a crazy world. I wish I could just disappear, find somewhere undiscovered, away some place in the middle of nowhere, you never know what's coming next, wars, wars, wars, invasions … and now with the technology the monsters have…" stopping, crying for a moment, wiping her eyes with her obviously-not-too-clean apron, "I have an extra room I'd be happy to give you for the night."

"Not 'give,'" Miriam corrected her, "Of course I'll pay."

"And, of course, that's fine."

Coming out from behind the counter, motioning to Miriam to follow her into her house at the back of the shop, all very antiquish-looking, Miriam wondering just how long it had been there, all the furniture looking very antique, hand-carved, fancy, fanciful lamps, rugs, although there was a nice big television in front of a hand-carved sofa in the living room, China lamps, shepherds and shepherdesses, Louis XIV-ish clothes, men with knee-socks, trousers that stopped at the knees, women in huge, billowy dresses, courtly and lush, with fancy shades that looked like they should have been discarded a hundred years ago, following her down a corridor to a back bedroom, canopied bed and matching dresser.

"*Tout est très joli, très, très joli* / Everything is beautiful, very, very beautiful."

"You're from…?" the bakery woman suddenly all curiosity, a face like an exploratory rat or weasel.

"From Israel originally, but then I converted to Catholicism and…"

"And then all this madness!'

"My two sons were killed. I just couldn't stay in Paris."

"And you're going?"

"I don't know … just going for the sake of going."

"Well, you'll be fine here tonight anyhow. And my name is Madame Gervaise, Anna. I'm a widow. My husband died from cancer. Two years ago. You tell me why! Out here in the country, we couldn't be closer to nature," looking up at and beyond the ceiling, "YOU tell me why!"

Waiting as if she expected an answer.

Just a little wind. Snow in the air. Miriam had expected it to be warmer as she went south, but…

"OK. I'll let you alone. If you need anything…" going over and fluffing up the duvet. "Good quilt, warm, warm, warm. Let me show you where the bathroom is," as she left, stopping and giving Miriam a little kiss on the cheek, a little hug, as if she were making her part of her family now, Miriam wanting to ask her about children, if she had them, where they might be, but let it go at that.

Followed Anna down to the primitivish bathroom, already dark outside, Chanukah-Christmas looming up in the distance, Christ the sun-god dying and being reborn after the winter-solstice, crazy how it all worked so beautifully cyclically.

"I suppose I should ask you how much…"

"*Demain, demain* / Tomorrow, tomorrow."

Like she didn't want to even think about it.

"Goodnight then Anna."

"Goodnight … *comment t'appelles?* / Your name?"

"Miriam."

"*Alors* … Miriam … sleep well."

"That shouldn't be a problem."

And she was off down the hall, and suddenly Miriam felt at home, like she was a kid again, back in Israel, back in Nineveh, back in ancient Egypt, back, back, back into something comfortably primitive, folding in around her like a soft wool (acrylic) blanket, *chez moi,* at home.

Took a couple of skullcap pills, bowels working surprisingly normal, bladder the same, a little washing, but not too much, her voices inside her whispering, "Leave the wounds alone, let them heal, heal, heal," then walking back down the cold hallway into her room, feeling like she'd stepped back in time into a more gracious, welcoming, accepting era, thinking of all the years and years and years that the Jews and Arabs had been fine together, two hands on the same body, remembering the time when Jews could have more than one wife, just like the Muslims, why all the madness now, remembering how Mohammed had always praised Abraham, their common ancestor … one God … *Melech Haolam* / King of the Universe.

Pulling on a stretch acrylic dress that was a perfect nightgown, as soft as dandelion-puffs, but warm, stretching around her legs as she got into the bed under a puffy obviously feather-filled (a feather here and there sticking out) duvet after she'd put a little melatonin tablet under her tongue and turned the light out and cautiously made her way over to the bed in the dark. Eyes like a cat. Almost instantly adjusting to the darkness.

Luxury. Ritzy. Smiling to herself when she remembered that the word "ritzy" actually came from a guy named Ritz, remembering one time when she'd gone to Boston with her husband on one of his business trips and they'd stayed at a Ritz Hotel. Off of Boston Commons, wasn't it? The US always a symbol of invulnerableness, n'est ce pas, until now, when unspoken, unspeakable threats hung over the whole world like the darkest, most threatening clouds.

Crying for a moment thinking of the menacing clouds over everywhere these days, now even over France, but not here, not here, not here.

Talking to herself, "I'm happy, however much time I have left, I'm happy now," loving to have her legs slowly warming up under the covers, pulling it around her shoulders, soft pillow, and dark, dark, dark, a small death, join them all for a while, parents and aunts and uncles, husbands and children and the hundreds and hundreds of generations of The Dead, Jews and Gestapo, Arabs, Philistines, Egyptians, pharaohs and emperors, as if Death were the only ultimate reality, not eternal life, but eternal nothingness, dust to dust and skulls to skulls … to (ultimately) dust. Would there ever be a time when Man was no longer on the earth at all, mankind and animal-kind, when there wouldn't be an earth at all, but just space, endless space, or would that shrink up into a tiny ball and die too, and all it would be would be Nothingness, zero, blank?

Then 'out' and starting to dream. Maybe it was the melatonin (1 milligram) that she'd taken, dreams of her two boys, and other boys (and girls) she'd never had, but had always wanted to have, some sort of endless celestial playground filled with swings and slides and volley courts, ramps filled with skateboarding kids, and she was there on a swing, back and forth, not an old (aging) lady but a kid again, up and down, back and forth, sky-earth, sky-earth … the kind of eternity she'd always longed for.

Waking up, her face all wet with tears.

Afraid to go back to sleep again, but then (settling back) … her voices inside her starting to whisper, *You are home here, this is where you should always have been, should always be, forever, and forever, haolam, olam, eternity, the universe, the eternal universe, and you part of it eternally, once you have been you will always be, be, be…*

88

The best sleep she had in years, woke up in the morning to the smell of baking bread, loving the bed, not wanting to really get up at all, bright sun, just a sprinkling of snow outside, thinking that she ought to ask the owner of the bakery for a job, or just stay in this room, or buy some little house in the town, really learn French, fit into this town, become a (slightly scarred) monument here.

But then, after washing (no shower, just an antique bathtub with elaborately carved claw-feet that looked like it belonged in a bath-things museum) and putting on her makeup, looking at her sewed-up wounds as she got dressed, heavy tights and heavy black suede lace-up shoes, thinking that another week and she could cut off the stitches, another couple of months a little makeup and the scars would disappear, she healed well … easily.

Then into the bakery.

"*Bonjour mon amie!*"

"*Bonjour … bonne journée.*"

Anna looking all bright and fresh, coming from behind the counter and giving her a hug and a kiss.

"So you look all rested!"

"Wonderful sleep!"

"And for breakfast…?"

Looking at all the breads and rolls, croissants.

"What I'd like, and I say it apologetically, humbly, as humble as I can make it … what I'd like is a roll and peach jam … impossible, no?"

"With me nothing is impossible," laughed Anna, "I'm a magician." Going into a little cupboard behind her, a little 'window' in the middle, covered with wire mesh, so very French, taking out a round, flattish jar of peach jam, picking a roll out of the case in front of her, a plate, cut the roll and scooped it full of jam, poured a cup of coffee from the pot next to the cash register, lots of cream and sugar, so that it would be more like coffee candy than just coffee itself, everything on a little wood tray with brass handles, brought it over to a table in the back.

"*Ça suffit*? / That's enough?"

"Wonderful," almost slipping into Yiddish … as if she were back with her grandmother, feeling like she'd always been there, as if the breakfast and all the rest of it would go on forever and forever, customers coming in, noticing her, smiling, realizing it wouldn't take long, long at all before she'd be part and parcel of the town, accepted, invisible. Or maybe a little visible, but not much. She was darkish, dark-haired, looked French, *could* look French, kind of nicely within the limits of the genotype, the jam delicious, filled with huge chunks of peaches, feeling it was almost like a miracle that Anna would have at hand exactly what she longed for, eating slowly, talking to Anna between customers.

"It's delicious. Never better."

"We've got to do something right, *n'est ce pas?*"

"As far as I can see you do everything right!"

"Now that's what I like to hear!" Anna coming over and sitting down with her. "I've been so lonely since my husband died, my children in Marseilles, Toulouse, that's where the jobs are, nothing much happening around here."

"This is happening!" Miriam answering her, holding up the remaining morsel of her roll, just one more bite left, although she felt she could have eaten half a dozen of them.

Feeling *so* good, in the here and now, *être, être, être*, being, being, being, expanding out into the bakery, entering into Anna's soul and seeing the world through her eyes, loving the medievalness of the town, some place that escaped the madness of the twenty-first century, primitive, back to roots, origins, sanity.

And then two little boys walked by outside, wearing little school-caps, carrying books, and suddenly her only two little boys were there sitting at the table, talking to her, *I want some of that bread ... and that jam, everything smells so good, good, good...*

And suddenly it all collapsed inside her.

Was going to stay on with Anna indefinitely, get old here, start working in the bakery, expand the bakery into a bigger restaurant, get it in the tourist guides, although there wouldn't be so many tourists fooling around in France from now on, would there, like the street-vendors in Jerusalem, no tourists, no vending, and who in their right mind was going to go to Israel with the threat of mad bombers lurking around everywhere?

Now suddenly decided to just leave. On the edge of tears. Fighting it back. Anna picking up on it.

"What's wrong? The coffee? Jam?"

"Nothing. I was just thinking about my dead sons, killed in Notre Dame when it was bombed, and my husband in Tel Aviv … all my family dead now."

"So stay here, I'll be your family, sister, whatever … it's not heaven, but close to it. I'd rather be here than anywhere else on earth. And you … we get along so well … I'm very much alone too."

Coming out from behind the counter and embracing her, Miriam embracing her back, but the voices within her still insistent, *get outta here, get moving, the only thing in life you have to embrace is death itself!*

"I have to leave, though. Let me get my things, and I can pay you, is a credit card OK?"

"I don't have any, you know, credit-card thing. It's a simple town. We could go to the bank, but…"

"OK, let me get my purse. I have cash."

"But…"

Anna starting to cry now, Miriam reacting to her crying by crying too, but still undeterred in her purpose, going back to her room, thinking of it already as *her* room, getting her things together, putting on her coat, purse over her shoulder, let anyone try to grab that and she'd show them, Anna sitting down now, having a cup of coffee, sad beyond sad.

"So how much do I owe you?"

"I feel like saying nothing, nothing at all. Or the world. You owe me the world … for leaving the way you are," taking a piece of paper under her saucer and pushing it over to Miriam, Miriam thinking *What a hypocrite you are, Anna, 'nothing at all,' and now you have it written on a piece of paper,* but just paying it, giving her a tip as well, then out to her car, another embrace, one last smell of the bakery, all the sauces and spices mixed in with the strong, heady coffee.

"*Au revoir* … come back…"

"You never know."

Down to her car, cloudy out, the threat of snow, used to being surrounded by TV, radio, short wave, listening to Israeli radio from time to time, enjoying showering in her own language. So few cognates between Hebrew and French/Latin...

For a moment, as she got in the car, uncertain about which way was south, then figuring it out, the sun barely, barely, barely visible up beyond the clouds, something inside her pushing her south like dragons pushing against her back, pushing her southward, as if there would be some answer in the south, some conclusion, resolution, revelation.

Getting in the car. One-quarter of a tank left.

OK.

South ... as if she were driving into the mouth of some dragon, universe-devouring God.

* * * * * * * * * * * * * * * * * *

Had found a petrol station at the edge of town, and as she moved further south, the clouds began to thin out and it was almost sunny, just on the edge of sunny, slowly, hour after hour, the landscape beginning to change, get primitive, wild, all sorts of evidence of ancient volcanic activity, mounds and mountains, humps and craters of long, long dead volcanos...

Which spoke to her:

"This is where you belong, where the gods died and the earth went crazy, back to the beginnings, *in principio Verbum est,* in the Beginning the Word is, only what is the Word *really* about, Null, Nihil, Nothingness, Nada ... *in the beginning was Nothingness, and Nothingness was Chaos, and out of Chaos Chaos was born, and Chaos lives on ... on ... on...*"

Nothing but chaos, everywhere all over the world, the ten commandments, the ten thousand mitzvahs shattered, scattered, surrounded by death, death and nothing more than death.

No idea where she was.

The sun twenty degrees above the horizon now, finding a road up to the top of this jagged, ragged mountain, a castle-like formation on the very top, a little village at the bottom, hardly anyone on the streets, the usual kids, an old woman with a babushka who would have been in a nursing home anywhere else in the world, barely making it along, Miriam *feeling* the creaking and cracking of her bones as she walked, carrying, what? Bread, of course, some legumes, onions … wondering how old she was, in her nineties…

And why did sea-turtles live three hundred years when we seldom made it beyond ninety?

Finding a place to park her car, getting out, the castle-like rock up above her now, bright beige in the light of the sinking sun, the old lady carrying her two bags approaching her now, not noticing her, but coming her way, her eyes down on the ground, concentrating on each step, avoiding slipping on the rock-paved street which was tricky walking for anyone.

"*Madame, c'est possible aller sur la montagne la?* / Madame, is it possible to go to the top of the mountain there?"

"*Oui, il y a un chemin* / Yes, there's a path." Pointing up ahead of her, adding, "*mais c'est très tard* / but it's very late."

"*Pour moi, non* / Not for me."

Smiling. And the old lady smiled back at her, going toward where she had pointed, finding what looked like a path up to the top.

Crazy to go up there, now? Too shadowy, although not that cold, really, another crazy little perfect village, why not just find a place to eat and sleep again, or go back to Anna, stop, rest, get old and die, why rush things?

Only her voices wouldn't let her alone:

"I command you to go up to the top of my castle, thousands and thousands and thousands of years of people here after I had formed its majesty, paleo, paleo, paleo, paleo, ancient, ancient, ancient, ancient … why should you live on now that all your loved ones have been killed? The terror is everywhere, and if it doesn't seek you, then you must seek it!"

Feeling, on all her deepest levels, that she wanted to die, for all the deaths, for the senselessness of life itself, bee, ant, spider, gnat, human, a moment in the light and then…

Starting up. Not an easy climb, but she could do it.

No one else around, as if the whole world, indeed, was dead. No sounds but the wind, starting to get winded, so out of shape, in a way loving it all precisely because it was so desolate, impossible, alone, just her and her personal dragons, how could the universe just have 'happened,' begun from nothing and then just formed, solar systems and planets, oxygen and amoebas, monocellulars, multicellulars, bugs, frogs, mammals … wanting a Voice out there somewhere, a Face, an *Adonai*/ God, *Melech Haolam* / King of the Universe, not just endless unexplained space within space within space. And if the universe wasn't infinite, what was it contained *inside of*? At the same time how could it just go on forever and ever and ever. Feeling that God was impossible, the universe impossible, her own life impossible, the mountain she was climbing…

Some hikers coming down from the top passing her by.

Americans.

Smiling at her.

"*Ça va?* / How's it going?" "*Bonjour* / Good day," "*Fait froid!*" / It's cold."

Horrible accents.

Answering them in Arabic.

"Salaam!"

"What was that, man? Salami?"

"Don't ask me, man…"

As she passed them laughing to herself, the first time she'd laughed for months. Maybe she should just look at it all as one cosmic joke, live with it, flow with it, go with it, life and death, who knows if she was really alive, or was it all illusion, or had anyone really died, or…

Then the voices inside her, all around her talking again.

"No more for you, time to join your own collective Past, they're all waiting for you in the Bowels of Death that have mistakenly been called Heaven. You'll see, see, see just how 'heavenly' they are…"

Laughter twisting through the wind, boa constrictors of diabolical laughter, feeling 'presences' there in the clouds around her, the rocks and stones themselves all devil-shit, devil-gall-stones…

Was she going crazy, or was this *Reality*, for the first time manifesting itself in her life?

In her life. In her death.

Struggling to the top, for a moment wondering if she was full of infections, meningitis, whatever, then the voices, this time like bubbling boiling water answering her thoughts,

"This is the first time you have ever heard The Truth,Truth, Truth…"

Having to stop for a moment and recover her breath, then starting out again. No one else around, and she couldn't believe how cold the wind suddenly was. Sweating, of course, but … starting climbing again.

On the very top now looking out at the vast fields below, feeling the presence of The Ancients now, whispering from the clouds *Join us, join us and our dead horses, join us and our dead horses…*

Dead horses?

Looking down over the edge and a sudden vision of horses being driven off the edge to their death by The Ancients.

Sitting down, wiping her forehead with her sleeve, as other voices started to whisper to her, as if from inside her heavy, padded jacket.

"Mummy, don't die, we live through you, we are your eyes and your skin, your voice and hair, when you eat, we eat, when you breathe, we breathe…" then another voice, deeper, bass, "They're right, sweety, me too, you'll be here soon enough, but live it out, Thou Shalt Not Kill, including yourself … or us … again…"

Her long-dead husband.

Going crazy?

But wasn't it crazy to jump down off the edge too?

More sounds around her, behind her, thundering, whinnying horses, throwing herself down on the ground and letting their ghosts gallop over her, crawling over to the edge and seeing them there below her, all tangled and broken, dying, and out of the bushes and trees men with spears killing them off, blood everywhere, thinking how horrible it would be to eat horse meat. Only why?

Crazy to kill herself, *n'est ce pas*?

Sitting down for a moment, wanting to somehow merge into the rocks themselves, into the fields below, the setting sun, pantheistically wanting to break off a piece of rock and eat it like Passover bread, drink the water in a little pool next to her feet like Passover wine, passing over, not into the Holy Land but into the Holy Universe, as if it all were the flesh and sun-eye, star-eyes of God. Actually stretching out for a few moments and sleeping, then up on her feet, down the mountain again, a lot easier this time, although the shadows kept getting treacherously longer, dark and more concealing, almost twisting her ankles and falling a few times, but it was as if the hand of God were leading her on, down, back into town, finding her car, first impulse to just get inside it and sleep there, but instead taking her suitcase and carrying it along with her, finding a little restaurant, going inside, restaurant-bakery, an old lady behind the counter, thinking (*triste, triste, très triste* / sad, sad, very sad) about Anna, wishing she'd just stayed there, you find a place you're gloriously comfortable in, why not just stay there.

The old lady coming over to her. Tiny little aristocratic face. Like something out of the aristocratic French past.

"Pretty empty around here these days … let me give you a menu."

"I don't need a menu," Miriam protesting, "just a sandwich of some kind, some meat, one of those beautiful, crusty rolls…" pointing over to the display cases filled with nice crunchy breads and rolls.

"Corned beef?"

"Fine."

"OK."

Smiling, going back behind the counter and picking out a couple of rolls, into the kitchen, you'd think there would be a radio on somewhere, a CD, a little music. But nothing. *Rien.* Getting hungry was so psychologically therapeutic, *n'est ce pas?* All of a sudden you're starving and you're sane. Coming out with a beautiful corned-beef sandwich, just a little sauerkraut in it. A Reuben sandwich. Crunched into it.

It couldn't have been better. Although what Miriam *really* loved most was a kibe sandwich, a street-vendor in Tel Aviv or Jerusalem, kibes, falafel, couscous, Arab-Israeli heartland food.

But this was so 'odd' to get a Reuben. Was the old lady a Jew, had she *been* a Jew, Jewish family now hidden in total 'Frenchness'?

"How do you like it?"

"Beautiful."

"I thought … I picked up the Israeli accent."

"So you're a…?"

The old woman shushing her.

"You never know…"

Miriam respecting her secretiveness.

"I need a place to stay the night."

"I have extra rooms. My husband is dead, one daughter in New York, another in Toulouse…"

Miriam laughing to herself. Was this some kind of pattern, widow bakery-restaurant women all over southern France?

"OK. Sounds good. I've got my bag with me."

"Nothing luxurious."

"And how much…?"

"We can talk about that later. I appreciate the company. In the summer this town is filled, filled, filled, the Roche de Solutré attracts all sorts of tourists. Tens of thousands of horses found at the bottom of the rock, going back, back, back ten thousand, twenty thousand years ago. They used to drive the horses off the edge of the cliff, they think, and then eat them."

"So the name of this town is…?"

"You don't even know?"

"My two boys were killed in the terrorist attack on Notre Dame. I left Paris and…"

The old lady looking at Miriam's face closely.

"It looks like you were…"

"Everyone in the church was."

"Such a tragedy."

"Madness."

"Is that all life is, war, then a little peace, things get good, then war again…"

An old man coming in the door.

"*Bonsoir, Cécile.*"

"*Bonsoir, Claude,*" getting up, going over to the counter, picking out two big fat loaves of bread and putting them in a bag for Claude, talking to Miriam as if Claude weren't there at all, Miriam all involved with her own hallucinations for a moment, the 'dream' she had had, the 'vision' of horses galloping toward her, as if her mind had all sorts of keys in it to unlock the ancient past, as if she were some sort of special visionary, shamaness, prophetess, "He always gets the same thing."

"Routine. It's a wonderful thing to be a slave to..."

"It's what I need," said Miriam.

"She was in Notre Dame when it was blown up!"

"I wouldn't go near Paris. Ever, ever, ever. If I could I'd go to the South Pole ... another planet ... who knows what comes next!"

"Agreed," said Cécile, "although I don't think anything will ever happen here."

"A lot happened ... the horses..."

"But so long ago."

"As if history didn't come around again."

Laying his money down on the counter. No change.

And with a wave to Miriam and Cécile, he was out the door.

"When I was up there," Miriam started confessing to Cécile, "I had ... I don't know what to call it ... a vision."

Cécile dismissing it.

"What isn't a vision? I take melatonin at night to help me sleep, and sometimes I don't know what planet I'm on..."

"But are you Jewish?" Miriam asked, then was sorry she had. A little discretion, just a *petite peu / little bit...*

"Southern France. Well, you'll see. It's much more 'Mediterranean' than the North. All kinds of 'influences' over the centuries. And for all the attempts to 'normalize' it from the North. We didn't even speak French here but Oc."

"Oc?"

"You'll see. Are you going to Toulouse?"

"I don't know where I'm going. I'm lost."

"Well, aren't we all. Just being here is enough to make you lost. I mean here, this planet. And now the madness again, like when the Moors occupied Spain and Constantinople and Indonesia, like they were going to take over the whole world. And if they did, would there be peace then? There would always be factions. What I try to do is mind my own business, keep it as 'primitive' as possible, although that's getting harder and harder with computers and the internet and cable TV, and

… what I love is flowers and sausage and Roquefort cheese and walks in the country, old, medievalish houses, the further back the better … *In the Beginning* … the spirit of God moving over the waters…" starting to cry for a moment, allowing herself the luxury of crying, giving in to her emotions, then pulling herself back, back into the Now, "come on, let me show you your room. Nothing elaborate. But be careful with the china," smiling snobbishly, "nothing more recent than the eighteenth century. I collect things, my mother collected things, my grandmother and great-grandmother…"

Miriam following her back down an ancient hallway that creaked as they walked along it, back to a bedroom looking out on a huge backyard that was all grassy, slightly snow-touched slopes, big old trees off safely away from the house, but still giving it all a beautiful sense of 'country,' or, like she'd said, 'primitive.'

Like looking out on a Monet landscape. Giverny.

The room itself totally quaint, from the ruffled, lace curtains to the big, four-poster bed covered with an understated, pastelish old quilt to the hand-carved dresser and its ancient mirror that needed 're-mirroring,' to the hand-carved armoire in the corner, all the old, old photos on the walls, one super-realistic painting of the mountain Miriam had climbed up on.

"Unsigned," said Cécile, "but it could be anyone … impressionism…"

"Who can say."

"But I love it, don't you?"

"I love all the landscape around here. It's like a green version of Israel."

"So I'll just leave you alone. There's a primitive bathroom down the hall. Somewhat updated. But years back. If you wait long enough everything gets primitive again." Smiling. "I'm practically prehistoric myself, by now…"

"And I'm getting there too…"

"Just a kid."

"See you later."

"Maybe I'll just lie down for a few minutes. After all that climbing."

"*A bientôt.*"

Closing the door more gently and carefully than she had to.

Lying down on the bed after a quick look in the mirror.

Feeling like she was back, back, back in time. Simpler times. Not that there weren't wars, man was war, conflict, murder, territorialism, power-grabbing, but in a moment of peace between wars, away from the current madness, old walls, old chandelier, the quilt warm.

Just a moment, a moment, and she'd go out and explore the rest of the town, then…

Toulouse, Toulouse, Toulouse kept ringing in her mind.

Something Father Peguy had said one day to her when he was talking about Richard Morris: "I wrote to him via his publisher … and he was very responsive, said he loved 'fans,' wrote in a kind of horrible, broken French which, nevertheless, was better than my English, said he always had wanted to move to France, not the north, though, nothing to do with Paris, but Toulouse, had this idea that if Toulouse had been the capital of France, if the French kings had been defeated by the Counts of Toulouse, it would have been a whole different country, more 'Mediterranean,' more exotic, more international … and, who knows, he may have been right. Although, believe it or not, I've never been to Toulouse. I'm very provincial, very Parisian. Parisian-English. Love London. *L'histoire, l'histoire, l'histoire…*"

Toulouse.

Closing her eyes and almost instantly beginning to dream of the Romans invading France (Gaul) in ancient, ancient times … *Omnia Gallia ist divisa in Tres Partes … all Gaula is divided into Three Parts … images of Roman ruins, temples and amphitheatres, houses … ancient countrysides and ancient ruins as if there were something in her that wanted to go back even further than the Romans, God the Mother, Mother Earth before the bearded gentleman in the skies took over, Earth as juice, breasts, womb, fertility, hills, trees, vistas, temples, even more romantic in ruins…*

VIII

Miriam's first impression of Toulouse, driving along the river, new apartment building after new apartment building, everything super-modern, chic, more like Hong Kong or Tokyo than anything in France, was that it was depressingly 'new.' She was so used to history herself, walking streets and going to temples that went back, back, back centuries, millennia...

But then, after being there for a week, she began to discover all the old churches and old parks, Roman ruins, and slowly she was more at home than she'd ever been before.

Ruins.

And not like Paris, everything fixed up and doctored into newness, but still emanating The Past, The Past, The Past.

Cécile in Solutré had given her her daughter's name and address, and she'd helped her find an apartment just next to the Garonne River, the Pont-Neuf, which was almost a duplicate of where she'd lived in Paris, on Cité, next to the Seine, close to another Pont Neuf, which meant 'new,' but which always really meant the oldest 'pont'/bridge in town. Forgetting the names of the bridges in Paris already, forgetting Paris itself, beginning to forget all the horrors that had been visited on her, feeling guilty about forgetting anything at all, but forgetting anyhow.

Like Sophie, Cécile's daughter, had said to her one day over coffee and meringue cookies filled with little chocolate chips, "You forget here, a hundred and sixty parks, the past still more present than any other place I can think of ... except maybe Prague ... or Vienna..."

"Oh, you've been to Prague and Vienna?"

"Of course. My husband and I. The kids stay with his mother in Muret."

"Muret?"

"Well, it's practically part of Toulouse now ... where the king in the north defeated the Count of Toulouse. You know ... the Albigensian Crusades and all that."

"I don't know anything about them."

"Well, you will ... might..."

Sophie living just a few blocks away, her husband, Émile, all curly black hair, looking very mediterranean, like a Syrian almost, Syrian or Yemeni. Three little girls.

"Will the next one be a boy?" Miriam asking Sophie one day.

"No nexts. I had a tubal pregnancy after I gave birth to Raymonda – named after Raymond VI – and I'm afraid to try for any more, even though I still have one tube left … it sounds so laboratory-ish, doesn't it?"

Sophie herself very 'mediterraneanish,' and the girls black haired and black eyed, with just a touch of yellowness, like olive oil, to their skin.

"I miss my boys so much. If I hadn't converted to Catholicism, if I hadn't been in Notre Dame at all, they'd still be alive today."

"If, if, if, if … that's all of history, isn't it?"

"I suppose so."

Tears in her eyes for a moment, but even in winter there was such a sense of 'green,' so much of a sense of 'forest' enclosing her, that she found it almost impossible to feel down for any length of time.

Feeling guilty for not feeling more sense of loss, for not feeling down most of the time, loving the look of the Capitole with its medievalish towers and the classic Parthenon-looking building at the back with its huge white columns … or the Romanesque-ish George-Labit museum with its white and red alternating patterns, looking very Moorish, like something in Lebanon or Syria, the Cathedral of St. Étienne, Notre Dame-ish but kind of 'squashed' together, long and narrow and elegant…

She found all kinds of North African Maghreb restaurants around town, where she could drink her peppermint tea and eat couscous and mutton stews, kibes, delicious little squares of halva, tiny little mantécous cinnamon cakes and gabelouz semolina cakes, for dessert, always thinking *there's no real conflict between Arabs and Jews, it's all invented by politicians, we're all the descendents of the same ancestors, salaam, shalom, what's the difference…?*

Loving the cafés in the older quarters of town, walking more than she'd ever walked before in her life, even on cold, windy days, thrusting herself into the special tastes of special coffees, the special tastes of special muffins and cookies, plumping up a little, buying a TV, getting cable, loving her room looking out on the river, feeling lost somewhere between the thirteenth and the twenty-third centuries.

Sophie became a close friend and they'd see each other almost every day, on leave from a nursing job in a local hospital, free time when the girls were at school or kindergarten. They'd go out for coffee, go to the flea market, sit in the park when the weather permitted. And she'd fill Miriam in on *l'histoire* … history of Toulouse:

"The South of France could have become a separate country. The counts of Toulouse were real rivals to the French king. Imagine two countries, France in the north and Toulouse in the south. Even a different language, Oc. And a different form of Catholicism … the Cathars, Albigensians … trying to 'purify' Catholicism, bring it back to its original roots … but the French, the 'North-French,' burned the Cathars. A place called Montségur, not far from here … the thirteenth century. Five hundred burned alive one day, and constant 'crusades' against the heretics, as they called them. That's why the churches and palaces here in the south are so impressive, the Toulouse counts had pretensions to take over the whole country. Or maybe not take over but just rule the way they wanted, create their own kind of 'purer' Catholicism... interesting, *n'est ce pas?*"

"Very interesting. Especially in the light of the Dead Sea Scrolls."

"So you've been reading, huh?"

"One of my worst vices."

"Virtues! I'm jealous. When I'm not involved with the girls, I'm either sickish or feeding Émile's desires. He's even turned on by my growing belly…"

Laughing.

Always laughing.

Very much in love with Émile, not just lovers but the best of, the closest of pals.

Miriam a little jealous, sometimes wanting a new husband, a little sex, feeling bad about 'taking care of herself,' which she did infrequently, and then not at all, found it very easy to just turn herself off entirely sexually, as if she were a hundred years old and had never had any sex in her life at all.

But still, when she saw Sophie and Émile together, like at lunch on a Sunday afternoon, she'd feel longing for someone, someone, someone to love, to talk to, touch and be touched by.

One favourite place she liked to go to in the afternoons was Le Palais, an old restaurant-bar down by the river close to her house. Have a little afternoon glass of black wine from Cahors, or some spicy raspberryish wine from Marcillac ... as always trouble sleeping, but the wines, she was convinced, helped her out at night. As did fish. Which she always tried to have at lunch.

Started buying books again, the more theological/historical the better, the older the better, sitting for an hour at least in Le Palais, sipping her wine and reading her books, getting more and more interested in the Cathars and their attempt to return to some sort of 'purified,' primitive Catholicism.

And she wasn't alone in the afternoons, either.

One old man especially a real 'wart' on the trunk of the afternoon's wine-drinking, her at one end of the dining room, him at the other. A weathered old guy with skin like a leather jacket, never quite fully shaved, but always with a few grisly, grizzly hairs sticking out around his sideburns/ears, always wearing a tweed cap and heavy tweed jacket that looked like they'd come from the Outer Hebrides a century older. Everything grey, grey, grey. Even a grey muffler-scarf around his neck. She always took her coat off when she was inside the restaurant, but not him, always sat huddled as if he was expecting an end-of-the-world blizzard at any moment.

After about a month starting to notice her, give her a smile, a little *bonjour*, which she returned, feeling lonesome at times, missing synagogues and Oneg-parties after services where she'd meet the old gang, Gorwitz and Horwitz and the Frankels and Shapiros and Ester Goldstein with her horribly poorly dyed red hair and little son who she was raising by herself after her almost-husband dumped her, and they'd sit and talk, open up, no holds barred ... *la raza*, the race, My People, understanding how, for thousands of years, the old Jews had survived/thrived in little villages here and there in Lithuania or Germany or Bohemia, Hungary, never a face you didn't know or didn't know you…

She was *beginning* to get to know grocers and butchers and bookshop owners, waitresses and waiters, but it wasn't the same, was it, she was the outsider, foreigner, stranger … getting less 'strange' all the time, but still outside the magic loop of ancient 'Frenchness.'

Then one day Mr Grizzley, after nodding a "Bonjour" her way, came over and stood shyly next to the table.

"*Est-ce que je peux…?*/ I wonder if I could…?"

"*Oui, oui … bienvenue* / Yes, yes, welcome."

Her French not quite 'cool,' but he sat down, uncomfortably at first, but then relaxing, lifting up his glass, smiling, her clicking her glass against his, as carefully as she could, afraid of breaking the glasses.

"*Lach heim!* / To life…"

Hebrew.

"But how did you know?"

"I have my ways," he smiled, then relaxed a little more, "I'm a pal of Émile's, he told me you're from Israel."

"That's better," she smiled, "I thought it was written all over my face."

"Not at all … around here you could 'pass.' Until you started talking…"

"Not quite there languagewise?"

"*Presque.* / Almost. Give it another year. French is such a gnarled, overpronounced language, not 'flat' like, say, Spanish…"

"You think Spanish is 'flat'?"

"Comparatively speaking," smiling, another Lach Heim, sitting back and *really* relaxing, if he'd put his feet up on the table she wouldn't have been surprised. "So how do you like it here?"

"Wonderful. Even in winter. But spring and summer…"

"It's the Bois du Boulogne times fifty, *n'est ce pas*?"

"Kind of … although I like Paris too. Now that there's no more kings." Laughing, finishing his dark, almost black wine, going up to the bar and getting another glass, no need for waiters with him, he was as much a fixture in the place as the tables or carefully crafted translucent windows, all made out of small parallelogram panes. "We have quite a history down here in the south ... which you probably know about, right?"

"A little..."

"A lot of historians try to make it a fight between the nobles in the south and the king in the north, but there was a lot more to it than that ... an attempt to return to, how shall I put it, 'true Christianity.'"

"In what sense 'true'?" Miriam suddenly very interested, the bar-restaurant disappearing altogether, the parks and gardens, Pont-Neufs and *capitoles*, St. Étienne cathedral ... it was as if they were out in the desert somewhere, next to some sort of mythical Dead Sea, he the Apostle, she the neophyte, disciple.

"You're a convert to Catholicism, right?"

"Y...y...yes..." not quite sure what she was a convert to, or even had converted *from*, in some sort of spiritual no-man's/no-woman's land of total doubt, scepticism, depression, not fear, but a sense of cosmic confusion.

"So look at the Virgin Mary. She can't have had sex with Saint Joseph, right? Jesus, the son of God, can't be born of just a woman, the father has to be the second person of the Godhead, the Holy Spirit, right? Does the Holy Spirit create a sperm to 'mate' with the Virgin's eggs? Or is Jesus just transplanted already foetal, into the Virgin's womb? The main thing is that sex is totally avoided, as if it were the worst of evils. Why couldn't the Holy Spirit have blessed Saint Joseph and turned one of his sperm into Christ, the Word, as in *The Beginning was the Word and the Word was God and the Word was with God...*"

"The Gospel of Saint John."

"Amazing!" reaching over and strangely, inappropriately, giving her a light kiss on the head, which, even more strangely, she enjoyed, thought of as right on track, appropriate. "But you see the main thing here is to totally avoid any connection between human sex, cohabitation, orgasms, insertions, The Flesh, and Jesus. And then, after he's born and grows up, the main point is that Jesus is totally supra-sexual. No sex with anyone, no sex of any kind. He is the Word made Flesh, but that's as far as the flesh goes. And then Catholic priests, they have to be celibate, *n'est ce pas?* The flesh is evil. Take the inscriptions in the catacombs viz a viz martyrs. It's good, great, wonderful to die, because you go to heaven, escape the flesh. The flesh is evil. Only why?"

"The flesh is evil, the spirit good. Very unlike Judaism."

"Bravo!" Again reaching over and kissing her on the head, like she was one of his pupils in some celestial school where head-kissing was an A, go to the head of the class, "And why is the flesh evil and the spirit good? Because the devil is associated with the flesh. An angel named Lucifer, the Light-Bringer, the Morning Star, rebels against God the Father and creates his own kingdom, the kingdom of the flesh, and Christ is born to bring us back to the spirit, so by being pure spirit we return to the original purposes of creation. The Catholic church talks about our bodies coming back to us on the last day, the end of the world, but we're spirits after we die, aren't we, ghosts, that's what ghosts are all about, we leave the flesh behind, and heaven isn't, excuse the word, 'fucking,' but beatitude, which means perceiving God, being closer to the Godhead, nothing ever mentioned about flesh, *n'est ce pas*? From the spirit we come and to the spirit we return, escaping from the satanic flesh. Well, that's what 'we' were all about here in the South, attempting to come back to 'original' Christianity, escape from the corruptions of the North. And what did the Catholics do to us?"

"Montségur. I was just hearing about/reading about Montségur, they burned five hundred Cathars at Montségur in the thirteenth century."

"Amazing!" Yet one more kiss on the top of her head, relieved that she kept her hair so clean, washed it twice a day, one of her obsessions, clean, clean, clean, clean hair. "You're already one of us!"

"Us?"

"Albigensians! Cathars! You don't think heresies 'die' just because you kill the so-called heretics, especially when the heretics are the real heroes of church history..." Suddenly and unexpectedly getting up, as if he were ashamed of spilling the beans the way he had, too much too soon, "*Basta!* I'll see you tomorrow, OK. If I'm still around..." looking up at the ceiling and beyond the ceiling, as if he were facing God himself.

Then out the door with one last wave, and when he was gone the guy behind the counter, a little waiter with black hair and a moustache who looked very much like Miriam's uncle, dead now for some twenty years from prostate cancer, smiled, came out from behind the counter, "Don't mind him. He's just lucky that they're not still burning people like they did here in the thirteenth century."

"You mean the heretics?" Drawing on her reading, too much reading, getting to be too knowledgeable about things she would rather have sidestepped to come into the Now, Now, Now, especially now that she was where she was…

"So you know about things?"

"*Un petit peu.* / A little bit."

"My philosophy has always been ignorance is bliss," laughing, going back behind the counter as an old woman came in with an empty plastic basket and the guy behind the counter started getting out some rolls and bread, muffins, without her saying a word.

Miriam finished up her wine, got a loaf of fresh bread for dinner, bread eater that she was, and butter, butter, butter, damn the calories and/or cholesterol, you're only a leaf on the tree of life once, and then eternal winter … maybe … maybe not…

Back to her place, the sun about thirty degrees above the horizon. Decided to take a little ride out into the country around Toulouse, just get away, have a little fun, not as far as Castelnaudary or Carcassonne, just out into the country a little, away from thinking and books and TV and films, just her and the *IT* that suffused and filled Nature, *whatever* it was all about.

Down along the river, that was her favourite route, even if the river sometimes got just a bit far from the road, farm fields are 'dead', asleep for the winter, the fields and then always the forests, *les forêts, les forêts, les forêts*, the wilder the better, sometimes the smaller roads canopied by trees even now, leafless, except for the pines, still full of their magic, something in her wanting to find the wildest, most deserted spot imaginable and just park and disappear into the forests, always fascinated by this instinct in her that wanted to escape from civilization altogether. Was that was 'evolution' was all about, developing from worms to people, still carrying within us three-toed sloths and dinosaurs, apes and skunks, instincts that pushed us back to what we really were, something just a wee bit different from orangutans and chimps, but still always longing to get lost in the forest-world that spelled out T-H-E D-I-V-I-N-E…?

Always amazed how anyone survived out in the wilderness the way they did, houses almost everywhere, although sometimes it seemed like just yesterday their ancestors were living in caves, like in Mas d'Azil with all its caverns and caves and Magdalenian harpoons and bones, coloured pebbles, which one day she'd seen when she'd visited the local museum, amazed that people had been there in that area from ancient, ancient times up to now, amazed always at the ancient churches and houses, medieval or baroque or whatever, amazed at how insanely persistent Man had always been everywhere, even after having spent most of her life in a country surrounded by ruins/remains that went back to what seemed Forever.

Then, just on the edge of dark, turning back north, back to Toulouse, a little sandwich for dinner, a little endive, some roast beef, some halvah, more wine, and then Canal Plus or Arte or La Cinquième, she subscribed to everything she could find, and loved to snuggle up in front of the TV in her snuggly pyjamas and dressing-gown, lying back on the softest sofa she could find, to hell with antiques and aristocratic taste, all she wanted was soft, soft, soft, warm, warm, warm. Was she becoming an alcoholic? Wine every day at dinner back in Israel, but always sacramental, a sacramental toast to Life, Life, Life…

Missing Hebrew sometimes, fantasizing-wishing – as she drove into her garage suddenly feeling tired beyond tired – that she could just drive back to Tel Aviv, or, even better, Jaffa, walk into Dr Shakshuka's in Old Jaffa with pictures of monkeys (like herself) all over the walls, and have some tomato-egg *shakshuka* or some *couscous*, her husband waiting for her with her sons, still kids, forever and forever kids, nothing changed … if there were ever anything like 'heaven' she could invent, it would be just that, home on the edge of the sea, hot, dry, exotic … and peace, peace, peace … not even wanting to read the newspapers or watch the news any more, feeling like she was back in the time of Mohammed himself when the Muslims moved out of North Africa on a wild holy mission of converting the whole world to their (true) faith, Spain, the Balkans, southern France, off into the South Seas…

Getting out of her car, walking out of the garage, dark now, thinking of nothing now but going to sleep, a little melatonin to help her dream/nightmare, neither dreaming nor nightmaring without a little chemical help, more asleep than awake … when suddenly she was startled by someone standing leaning against the wall outside the garage exit; having a sudden impulse to turn, run away, go back into her car and start driving to she didn't know where. Someone with a bomb tied to their stomach? They'd found out she was an Israeli and were going to get her! For a moment almost welcoming the idea that someone might blow her to kingdom come … if there were any kingdom to come to … just end it, Kaddish, the prayer for remembering The Dead suddenly rolling around in her head, *Yitgadal veyitkadash shemei raba…*

"I figured you've have to come back some time! Just standing here has got me into lots of troubles, almost-troubles anyhow … but it paid off…"

It was the grizzled guy from the café-bakery, who had walked out on her earlier in the afternoon.

"You really scared me."

"I'm sorry. I'm sorry I walked out on you this afternoon too. Maybe another hundred years and I'll get mature/civilized. I'm Paul Theroux. I used to be an M.D., made enough to kind of retire, become, what would you call me, a 'preacher,' although I like to see myself more as a 'helper.'"

Reaching out and waiting for her to shake hands. Which she did. Suddenly all her fears and tiredness and nostalgia gone, transformed into sudden human warmth, glad there was *someone* there waiting for her, sick of aloneness, loneliness, solitude.

"Why don't you come up for a little coffee or something?"

"You're not afraid?"

A little afraid, yes, afraid of everything these days, everything and everyone, as if there were a meteorite somewhere out there the size of Peru, just waiting to slam down on the head of

Mother Earth. But…

"Of what? You're not a vampire or zombie, are you?"

"No," he smiled, "I went through therapy, got cured … like a just-born bison these days."

"Bison?" She didn't get the reference.

"You know, buffalo."

"Buffalo?" Laughing. "Buffalos here in Toulouse?"

"I don't live in Toulouse," he said as he got into the lift behind her and she pushed her floor, 13, a lucky number for Jews, she didn't know exactly why, "but in The Great Beyond."

"And how's the weather there?"

"Perfect. Always perfect."

A little rough, the stop at 13, everything in France always a little 'rough,' she thought, under the sleek, perfect surfaces always on the edge of returning to *le primitif*. Like Israel in a way, always expecting a Sumerian to come knocking on your door.

Down the hallway, fumbling for her key in her just-a-little-too-worn-out leather over-the-shoulder purse, which, like her just-a-little-too-worn-out leather shoes, she loved too much to simply replace.

Standing back, letting him go in first.

Him noticing everything, everything, everything, the pictures she'd been buying, an iron(?)/lead(?) bust of Athena, an ancient menorah she'd picked up at the flea market, some of her own drawings, which she'd carefully framed … she was an obsessive collector, desperately missed all the things she'd left behind in Paris, but had never written to anyone to get them and send them to her, as if Paris were some sort of huge cellar door that she'd banged close with a big thud and would never open again.

"Beautiful taste!" Sitting down on a leather sofa in the living room, opposite her new Sony DVD-equipped TV, loving to watch old French films at night, like *Le Chat* / The Cat … something raw, super-real, almost brutal. Hating just one French film-maker, Jean Luc-Godard, because he never stuck to his 'subject,' if he even ever had one. "Very comfortable. It's dangerous, I'm almost 'here' and not in the Great Beyond."

"Here isn't always that bad," she smiled. "Coffee … or…?"

"Nothing with caffeine, I'm the world's worst sleeper."

"Ginger and red raspberry tea and some gabelouz?"

"Gabelouz, by all means," he said in super-seriousness, then smiling, "whatever they are."

"Semolina cakes with almonds."

"Exotic."

"Not really … for me … Israelis are exotic."

"Yes, I suppose so. But so are Toulousians … *nous avons notre histoire aussi* / we have our history too."

"Who doesn't?" she smiled, went out into the kitchen as he started playing around with the TV controls, managed to turn on the film she was currently watching, *La Séparation*, this frustrating film about a warm marriage turned cold, the wife trying unsuccessfully to warm it up again, a man-hating film that she kind of agreed with … against her better thoughts and inclinations.

Very lavish with her tea-bags, a ginger and raspberry bag in each cup, which she microwaved, got the gabelouzes out of the refrigerator and put them on almost-museumish looking plates she'd got at the flea market, plates that matched the cups, eighteenth centuryish, full of drawings of roses, the edges all scalloped and shaped and filled with carefully drawn gold lines. Wanted to give him more, a sandwich, a beer, some black, black local wine, but held herself in, deep down feeling very close to him, no fear, no restraints even.

Funny, she seldom warmed to anyone the way she had warmed to him. As she walked out with her goodies on a big platter, she very politically correctly switched off the film/TV, committing the room back to its usual utter quietness, except for an occasional boat tooting on the river, or the constant hushing shhhhhhush of the traffic on the street below, a honk once in a while, but very seldom.

"I'm so alone here," she said as she put down the tea and gabelouzes on the coffee table in front of the sofa, where she'd always put her legs up when she watched films, so comfortable that she hardly felt she had a body at all, was pure angelic spirit.

"No need to be alone," he said, smelling the tea, smiling, nibbling on a gabelouz, "very nice. I shouldn't say it but I feel very *chez moi* / at home here, very comfortable. And you don't have that usual French 'combativeness' about you that just *loves* trouble, thrives on conflict."

"I don't thrive on conflict. Not at all."

"But like I was saying, there's no need to be alone, you could become one of us…"

"Us?"

"I have to be careful how I define us," he said cautiously, but with just a little irony to his cautiousness, as if he were self-mocking, making a subtle undercover joke out of the whole thing, "At least they don't burn people any more. *Liberté* of speech and all that. The French Revolution wasn't all bad, believe me. Not like back in the twelfth century, they burned five hundred of us at Montségur…"

"They?"

"The Inquisition."

"Us?"

Sitting back, relaxing, getting quietly expansive, no rush, as if he were God creating the world and wasn't in the slightest rush.

"Put it this way, orthodoxy teaches that God controls everything, right? Judaism, for example … God brings up and brings down the sun and moon, revolves the world through the seasons, is always here, there, everywhere, a 'presence.' He's always talking to the prophets, *n'est ce pas*? And He's always talking to Jesus, the apostles … and later the saints … so what about blowing up Notre Dame or Vesuvius or earthquakes in the Andes or San Francisco, what about blowing up pizza parlours in Tel Aviv, innocents killed like ants being insecticided by a terrorist? Read the newspaper headlines. One of my favourite pastimes, to just browse at newspaper stands, the *New York Times*, *Le Monde*, of course, I can read enough German to understand the headlines on German newspapers, every day more nonsense, Moscow or Central America, Brooklyn. Does it look like The Divine is in charge of the world?" Miriam suddenly starting to cry as she sat down next to him, all the madness of the last few years in Israel running through like cold, freezing water, giving her the chills, reaching over and taking her cup of tea, a momentary impulse to just go into the bathroom and take a hot, hot shower, burn instead of freezing

113

... "I'm sorry..." him moving over closer to her, obviously wanting to put his arm around her and comfort her, but holding himself tactfully in, "I didn't realise just how close all this stuff was to you."

"It's practically all I think about. Try not to, but it's always there. That's why I immerse myself in French films and TV, never miss an opera, concert, recital, play. Art is kind of like cortisone cream to me, Haldol, Anti-madness..."

"Wonderful, wonderful," moving back away from her as she recovered her balance, "but let me tell you, we're a close-knit group, prudent, you know, not 'sneaky', but prudent," his mouth full of gabelouzes now, sitting back as if he'd never been anywhere else but here, this was home, *heimat, chez moi* forever and forever, *olam, olam, olam*, Amen. "The flesh is evil, you know that, 'desire', all the temptations of the flesh, the world one huge mass of sexual madness, fornication, adultery, abortion, masturbation ... and the only time you're really happy is when you're 'post-flesh', as close to pure spirit as you can get. Like in the catacombs of the early church, when Christians would get killed by the Romans, it was never a tragedy, but always a relief, a blessing, the end of earth, the beginning of heaven. I always like to think of myself as kind of a primitive Christian-Buddha, beyond the flesh, just waiting – happily – to be called to my eternal reward."

Miriam suddenly seeing in her mind, her father, mother, grandparents, brothers, sisters, all the 'pack' alive again, Passover, *LACH HEIM, LACH HEIM, LACH HEIM*, TO LIFE, TO LIFE, TO LIFE, never 'eternal rewards', but just one big, extended-as-long-as-possible, enjoyed-as-much-as-possible NOW. Then suddenly shifting, thinking of Death, all the deaths surrounding her, Israel living in constant fear of you never knew what, Israel, the US, Germany now, Russia ... the whole world made out of petrol, and maniacs out there with torches in their hands just waiting to set the whole damned, literally damned, thing afire.

"I know what you mean ... I've been through it."

"That's what I gather. Lucifer, the Bearer of Light, if not the equal of God, coming pretty close," becoming very 'sweet', like a father to her, an ancient Rabbi trying to get the flowers of joy to sprout in her heart for a change, instead of just being filled with endless wastelands of cactus and drought, "would you like to come to a service? Friday night … Sabbath-Eve … I can pick you up."

"Well … why not … what time?"

"We start at eight, the drive's about half an hour. Say seven, how about that?"

"OK. I'll be down in front at seven."

"Fabulous," finishing up the last little fragments of his gabelouzes, down to the last drop of his tea, as if he could have eaten whole bowls more and drunk a hundred mugs more too, getting up, walking him to the door, kissing her on both cheeks.

Out the door, her standing there watching him as he got in to the lift and waved goodbye, thinking how ironic it was that the one man she had really warmed up to since she'd arrived in Toulouse was Mr Anti-Flesh, spiritual castrati…

IX

Friday late afternoon, the sun just a few degrees above the horizon. That's how Miriam measured time, nothing to do with clocks, just dawns, days, dusks and darks. Even beginning to enjoy the dark itself, when she couldn't sleep, getting up sometimes and sitting on a dining room chair near the window that faced out on the river, just enjoying the river itself, the cars, trees, how the light would come into the room so she began to see almost as well in the almost-dark as during the day. *Les yeux d'un chat* / The eyes of a cat.

Doorbell rings.

She goes to the front window, opens it up, cold, cold, cold.

There he is looking up at her.

Waves. No words. No words needed.

Pulls on her heaviest (new) padded coat and a wool cap, purse, boots, down in the lift, out the front door, Paul all ironic guffaws and smiles when he sees her.

"I know it's not Israel, but it's not the Aleutian islands either!"

"Aleutian islands?"

"You know. Up by Alaska ... where the American Indians were supposed to have got to the New World."

"It's been years," she answered apologetically, embarrassed at not remembering it all, all, all...

"Imagine how you'll be at my age."

"No, that's too much for even my imagination."

Laughing. And he laughs back.

Out to his Volkswagen. One of the new bugs. A little sleeker than the old ones ... but not much. Him opening the door for her, with a little bow, old fashioned gallantry. Which she loved. Had been feeling *so* old-lady-spinsterish recently, as if her whole sense of youth and well-being depended on men catering to her, bowing to her, opening doors for her and telling her she was belle, belle, belle ... beautiful.

Not feeling cramped at all as he closed the door and got in the driver's seat.

"Isn't it a bit unpatriotic to have a German car?"

Kidding. But not really. Totally accepting German/the Germans, the 'new' Germans, at least superficially, but still never quite forgetting the holocaust, no matter how much she thought the thing through, going back before Hitler and convincing herself that all the slaughter of the Jews was Hitlerish and that if you didn't play the game you got shot yourself, which was why most people played it.

"Well, my dealer made a lot out of the deal too, look at it that way," he smiled as they took off through the busy streets, out of her medievalish, ancient-townish area into the more modern parts of town, not that different from Paris, or Tel Aviv, as far as that went, amazed sometimes at just how 'universal' things became on a worldwide basis, computers and video games and DVDs, the whole world becoming 'nerdsville' … and then a sudden image of Afghanistan coming into her mind … all those 'tribes' out in the middle of poppysville, still on the edge of pre-history…

"You Toulousians seem so radically involved with the past, the Inquisition, it's amazing…"

"What are you talking about, Toulouse is the centre of the aerospace and communications industry, it makes the rest of France look medieval … just look…"

True enough, driving along next to the new apartments next to the river now, all the cars and mad 'quickness' of the traffic, it was all futuristic, but…

"But…"

"No 'buts' about it, you just happened to fall into the hands of the real 'radicals,' although … in a way you're right too, under all the futuristic surface, *l'histoire est toujours ici* / history is always here … like an appendix or gallbladder scar. Or, the way I/we like to see it, a door into a purer Past, a purer Truth … sanity…"

"So how far do we have to go?"

"Not far. Forty-five minutes and we'll be there."

Reaching over and turning on the radio … no, not the radio … the CD player, this bombastic, super-emotional classical music blaring out, the sound-system just a little too good, realistic…

"I suppose I should recognize that." Feeling culturally

inadequate. A classical music buff, supposedly … but then there were all the worlds she didn't know a thing about, then suddenly a voice within her talking, her just repeating what it was saying, "Mahler … the Romantic Symphony…"

"Very good. You get an A."

Smiling. Happy.

"I've always been interested in the Austro-Hungarian empire, Vienna, Prague, Budapest … *Ich weiß nicht was soll es bedeuten das ich so traurig bin …*"

"Which means?"

"I don't know what it means that I'm so *atsuv*…."

Suddenly realizing that at the end she had stuck in a Hebrew word.

"*Atsuv* must be some French I've never heard before," he smiled.

"Oh, I'm sorry. A little Hebrew came walking in there. You know what that means, don't you? That I feel one hundred percent at home with you. My essential 'me' is starting to wiggle free."

"I feel the same way with you."

Feeling too much at home, in fact, feeling deep, deep levels down, that she'd always been with him, would always be with him, this was her place, forever and forever and forever, Amen, the Melech (King) and Maalka (Queen) of the universe…

Scary, squiggly, wiggly feelings that she was almost afraid of as they surfaced and started to breathe.

Just the music for a while. So sunny out, things beginning to sprout, get green again. No need for words, some sort of spiritual 'plasma' joining the two of them together now, both of them, without a word, sharing the same sense of the year's resurrection, her beginning to think about Passover without really wanting to, the whole sense of suffering ending in triumph, passing over (The Red Sea) into triumph against the Forces of Evil, as if it could happen again, God reappear after millennia of silence and suddenly create peace/*shalom* on earth again.

Overwhelmed at just how 're-beginning' everything felt, the landscape getting all rocky and mountainous again, almost feeling that she was back in Israel … and (yes), he was her long-dead husband resurrected, like Jesus coming out of the tomb and rising to heaven.

"Spring on the way, huh!"

Tears in her eyes, in her voice. Him looking over at her.

"So what are you crying about?"

"I'm goofy, I guess. I always cry when I'm happy."

"And I always laugh when I'm sad," he answered, laughing, then holding the laughter back, "Better watch out, I'm happy, no laughing, I'm quite happy, especially happy to have you as practically one of us."

"Always experimental. Curious as to what you're really all about…"

When the Mahler finished, he reached over to the glove compartment and took out a little package of the complete symphonies of Mahler.

"How about going through all the symphonies, number one on…?"

"Where are we driving to, North Africa?"

"Not much further now. But we can start with Number 1, OK?"

"OK."

Finding number one and putting it on, very slow, very 'rustic.'

"It's almost like country peasant dances," she said with a smile, "I love it."

"That was the whole point of the Austro-Hungarian empire, Dvorak's *Bohemia's Meadows and Forests* … sometimes I'd like to just go back there and die…"

"You've got lots of years ahead of you yet!" she said with what she thought sounded like stupid, unthought-out optimism the minute she'd said it.

"Prostate cancer, all that kind of stuff. Not too many more. I live on strawberries and vitamins, but … I'm all set for…"

Looking up at the bright cloudless sky, her wanting to say that she wished she believed in such things herself, but never had managed to make it … but not wanting to rattle his chandeliers … and besides, there was a small little girl part of her that *did* believe it all, heavens and hells and purgatories and limbos and whatever else you wanted to invent, anything but just the idea of it all ending like an erased poem, a snapped-in-half CD, wanting, in fact, to snuggle up against him, head on his shoulder, boyfriend and girlfriend it, feeling even more than ever the immensity of the indifferent, mindless Out There that no one could or ever would explain.

But staying where she was. He wasn't too 'inviting' was he?

No more words for a long, long while, just enjoying the hills and mountains, greening up now in the earliest of springs, wanting to just BE, BE HERE forever and forever and forever, forever and forever inside Mahler, inside the sunlight and the clouds, the old villages and clumps of trees, feeling for a minute that it all *was* God, the pantheists were right, everything that was was Divine ... *Baruch ata Adonai Eloheinu Melech ha'olam.* Not just king of the universe, but the universe itself.

Starting to cry again, just being, being there, as if it were all magic, illusion, it couldn't, couldn't really be happening, could it?

Him not noticing at first, but finally, when she took a handkerchief out of her purse, he looked her way.

"So what's going on now?"

"I'm simply happy. Mrs Contrary ... the happiest I've been in years..."

"Great. Wonderful. Maybe I should cry too, be 'normal' ... I'm happy too..."

Then, ironically, just a few more miles, and he turned into a driveway.

"Believe it or not we're here. I can be nasty to you so you can stop crying..."

"I'm fine," she said, dry-eyed now, curiosity getting the better of her sense of, what was the word she was searching for, *satori* ... curiosity about the huge villa up on this hill in the middle of nowhere, villa *and* garden, all beautifully landscaped, a whole bunch of cars in the 'car park' at the foot of the hill the villa itself was perched on.

"So many cars!"

"Well, there's quite a few of us ... you'd be surprised, in the midst of all this aerospace-computer nonsense that's going on around us, that there's still a few of us left who deal with REALITY!"

The word 'reality' almost angry. Which got rid of the rest of her tears, feeling spooky and eerie now, like she was walking into some sort of haunted house movie dream.

Mahler off. Just the wind in the trees as they walked up the beautifully carved iron-railinged marble steps to the front door of the house, expecting a doorman-butler wearing a white wig, long-tailed frock-coat and knee-breeches to be at the door, but no one was there at all, just open … inside, through run-down but magnificent halls, a dining room, living room, *salle de journée*, to the back of the house, down a series of ancient stairs into a huge, dome-ceilinged basement, candles in little holders all along the wall, a big altar up front.

Sophie, Cécile's daughter, sitting there as if she were waiting for them … all delight and effervescence when she saw them, like a huge glass of seltzer water.

"So you made it."

"Of course," he said, smiling.

Sitting down, the place still filling up.

Impressed by the altar, the rest of the 'congregation' … all looking very seriously nerdy, nerdy beyond nerdiness into solemnity as a way of life/death.

Music piped in. A cappella. All in – what was it, Latin…? Nothing she'd ever heard before, somewhere between requiems and heaven-songs, after-death solemnity, but very nicely done, wishing her eyes would just behave themselves as she began to cry again, quietly, unnoticeable, as long as no one looked her way, and no one did.

Then the music stopping and from a doorway on the side of the altar a 'priest' emerged wearing an elaborate hat, her thinking 'kipu,' something Eastern Orthodoxish, or like some very conservative Rabbis she'd seen in the old days in Israel, all black, a circle around the head and then 'puffs' of cloth, six in all, all gathered together at the top where there was a small silver cross. Bearded. Dark horn-rimmed glasses, wearing a long, black gown with a 'shawl' (tallit) around his shoulders all filled with writing in … it wasn't Hebrew, was it…? It was!

More tears.

Feeling she'd just stepped back a few millennia into some sort of sacred, sacred Past.

The music beginning again, the priest-rabbi coming down the aisle into the congregation, looking them all over, nodding, greeting, stopping in front of her and her friend.

"So I see you brought her, "holding out his hand, "welcome … as long as you're not from the CIA…"

"CIA?"

Didn't get it. Then did. OK … CIA … too many languages, cultures…

"*Je suis de Melech Haolam* / I'm from the King of the Universe."

Thinking, *he won't get the Hebrew, will he, but…*

"*Moi aussi…*" then adding in Hebrew "*Bli safek* / Without a doubt."

And nicely pronounced too, hardly Frenchified at all, but lots of slush and gutturalness to it.

Going on, greeting everyone there, Miriam amazed that he knew any Hebrew at all, feeling more at home than she had for months, years…

Then back up to the altar, breaking bread, putting it in two beautiful little reedish-looking baskets, two altar-girls, no! altar-women, bringing it down and distributing it to the congregation, everyone taking a little piece, back up to the altar, bringing down trays of little tiny paper-cups of wine, passing them out to the congregation too…

Bread and wine.

Whenever she'd gone to Mass she'd never missed the connection between Passover's bread and wine and communion bread and wine, but the way the 'priest-Rabbi' had torn the bread up, with zest and vigour, reminded her of the way her father had done it when she was a kid, every dinner every night beginning with the bread and wine ritual and a bunch of Lach Heims, Lach Heims, Lach Heims, whatever came after, so what, we were Here and Now and Here and Now were forever … as long as they lasted…

"Our Father who Art in Heaven, Hallowed be Thy Name, Thy Kingdom Come, Thy Will Be Done, on Earth as it is in Heaven…"

Which seemed just a bit too bland and straightforward for Miriam who had expected some sort of biblical fireworks, something new/impossibly old, fresh by *being* impossibly old…

The priest lifting his hands up, a signal for everyone to stand up. Which they all did, Miriam amused at just how, not exactly 'fat' they were, but 'ample,' all the coats off, but under them all this heavy winter wear, old tweed jackets on the men and wool dresses and *blousons* on the women, very few younger people, mostly oldsters, and she couldn't help but think that when they died off, who would carry on this message, this 'movement,' at the same time somehow finding them all *sympaticos* just because they were so 'ordinary,' unpretentious, 'real.'

"Oh, Lord, we who have sinned wish to confess our sins unto Thee, Our Great One, Adonai, Melech Haolam," Miriam surprised, almost startled by the use of Hebrew, *Adonai, Melech Haolam,* at the same time feeling even closer to them all than she had, "and we wish to confess our sins openly unto Thee, so that you might forgive us and we can start all over again, sins of the evil flesh, if anyone has eaten fish or flesh, in any way has become more attached to the body and this world instead of looking upward full time and anticipating the release of Death and entrance into Eternity … une, deux, trois…"

One, two, three and they all began together, filling the chapel with a cacophony of almost-screamed sins, Miriam hearing fragments here and there, something about "meatballs with my spaghetti," an old guy over to her right, long hair tied back in a ponytail, looking very weird, something about old Bardot films on DVD, evil thoughts, a very fat woman in a coarse, uncomfortable-looking red wool dress in front of her, something about enjoying her body too much, someone behind her about "*mon mari* / my husband…" from the fragments she was hearing coming to some sort of lightning judgement about the whole group and the thrust of their beliefs, totally anti-HERE, anti-THIS WORLD, something about "*platine laser* / laser disk players," the whole modern world was evil, all that counted was the Afterlife, this Life was nothing but steps leading up to the edge of an Abyss that you jumped off of into … ETERNITY…

Which gave her the chills, it was so undefined, bland, unknown, like jumping out of a plane into clouds…

Nuages, nuages, nuages…

Her impulse was to just leave, give Paul a kiss on the cheek and get out, go back to her apartment and watch TV, eat a ham(!) sandwich and some shrimp, play with herself sexually, sin and enjoy it, if sin meant Here, Now, Fun, and Virtue meant There, Never, Abstinence…

Only then the confession was over and everyone sat back down in the pews and the priest relaxed a little. He was old, uncomfortable standing up, reached over and pulled a tall stool behind the pulpit and sat down, something she'd never have dreamed of up on a *bima* / altar, amused that the Hebrew word had come into her mind first, 'bima' instead of 'altar,' probably because she was so at home here, thinking back to how it must have been in the Fiddler on the Roof days in the old Jewish towns in Bohemia or Lithuania or Russia or Germany where it was *all* friends, all one gigantic family…

"OK, my friends," the priest continued, more comfortable now, Miriam imagining just how much arthritis, how many back pains and joint pains and pains here and pains there that the old guy (first thinking, oddly, 'old saint,' correcting her thoughts) really had, "OK, my friends, how lucky we are to be who we are, where we are … more than once I've heard it said that we're just a dying remnant of the past, an almost-extinct breed, but tonight we have with us a new 'convert,' brought to us by Paul. I almost said 'St. Paul' … and I wonder if she might get up and tell us a bit about herself before we start the conversion process…"

Staring at Miriam. Simply stopping and staring. And everyone else in the congregation turning around and staring too. Like an extinct Eohippus had just walked into the room, a Stegosaurus, or something equally absurd … impossible…

Her wanting to just get up and run out, run away, try Israel again, become a Muslim and move to Tunis … Casablanca … walk into some dream bar and sit down at the bar next to Humphrey Bogart and Ingrid Bergman. The priest indicating for her to stand up.

She stood up, didn't flee, a million years of 'upbringing' in her keeping her fast in her place.

"Why don't you just tell us something about yourself…"

The old priest couldn't have been sweeter, listening to him was like eating halvah, baklava, bourmas.

She stood up.

"*Premier, je ne suis pas totalment 'chez moi' en français /* First of all, I'm not totally at home speaking French..."

"Neither are we," smiled the priest, "we'd prefer Oc, wouldn't we, my friends?"

The congregation all laughing, smiling, nodding yes.

Oc, Langue d'oc. Finding it difficult to imagine that anyone still spoke or even remembered the other ancient languages of Southern France, remembering one time, years earlier, when she'd been to Valencia, Spain, not too long after her marriage, a kind of second honeymoon, going into shops and everyone would be speaking some language she didn't understand a word of, instantly converting to Spanish when she'd walk in, Valenciano instead of Spanish, still spoken locally...

"Like Yiddish, when I was growing up. Hebrew was spoken and all, but my parents and their friends, when they wanted to feel 'comfortable,' always slipped into Yiddish..."

"So you are originally Jewish, from what I gather...?"

A look of incredulity spreading across all the faces in front of her. Disbelief, then ... what was it, distrust, rejection? Giving way to acceptance. She was what she was, *had been* what she *had been*...

"Originally from Tel Aviv ... Tel Aviv-Jaffa. Although I travelled a lot when I was a child, and after I got married. Studied French. U. of Tel Aviv, studied art, architecture ... then suddenly become Mum / *La Mère* ... full time. My husband was killed by a terrorist in a pizza parlour in Tel Aviv, and I 'went crazy,' moved to Paris, a permanent tourist..." stopping, *wanting* to just stop, sit down, implode in on herself, fold in on herself like a crumpled-up piece of paper, vanish, the image of throwing herself in front of a train passing through her mind, but she went on, "I started drawing the statues on Notre Dame, Sacré Coeur, other old churches ... I don't remember all the names ... and one day I met a priest from Notre Dame, we become friends, I converted to Catholicism, was very happy 'inside,' like I'd turned a page of history, got 'modernised' or something. I was living with my two sons on the Île San Luis

125

and one Sunday at mass I was at the Communion rail in Notre Dame, my sons in the back, still Jewish, but I was bringing them with me just to give them a chance to have contact with Catholicism, and…"

She stopped, didn't want to, but couldn't help it, just confessing it all openly this way made it as if it were happening again right there in front of her, remembering their mangled bodies in the morgue, her having to identify them … and then her madness … fleeing down here to … this other kind of madness…

Paul standing up, her pal.

"They were killed in the bombing of Notre Dame."

"I understand, we all understand," said the priest, all empathy and sympathy, as if he were inside her, seeing it with her eyes, feeling it with her feelings, "and many thanks for your telling us what you did," Miriam sitting down, not even crying, as if she were paralysed, totally neutralized by her grief, the priest continuing on, "all the 'traditional' talk about God controlling the world, the sun in the morning and the moon at night, the beauty of the human body, the thrills of 'the flesh,' beautiful breasts versus breast cancer, beautiful joints versus arthritis, sea turtles living three hundred years and we barely make it to, what, seventy, eighty, ninety. I know myself, when I go to bed at night, after all my prayers and pills, I lie there, I'm eighty-one, you know, I lie there and think about one thing, everything ending, the night, the clouds, the trees, a little glass of wine every day at dinner, my love of the hills here in the south, the undulating landscape, feeling I'm some sort of impressionist who simply doesn't paint, or put it into music, like, say Debussy … ein, zwei, kaput … if I may be allowed a little German … but then heaven opens up, I fall asleep and I'm finally released into eternity, God the father, God the Son, God, the Holy Spirit, and there I am, up amidst the clouds talking to Jesus, 'So you finally escaped from the filthy, temporary, but necessary flesh, and made it up to my … our … kingdom,' the body good but for one thing … to be got rid of, dumped, discarded, so that the spirit can be released and go to its true home … heaven … something the early Christians knew so well, inscriptions in the catacombs, which I have seen, glad that their children or wives or husbands were killed by the Romans because they had been released from the flesh and were finally THERE, UP THERE where they really belonged. This world, this horrible lower world, controlled by Lucifer and the other demons who control this world and cause its floods and earthquakes, volcanic eruptions, our cancers and oedemas and Parkinson's Disease, lymphomas, strokes, the flesh, the flesh, the flesh, evil, evil, evil … waiting, waiting, waiting to die and be released from evil and step into eternal bliss … so I understand what you have gone through, are still going through, my friend," looking out at her in the darkness of the congregation, Miriam somehow feeling comfortable, that old back-in-the-village feeling again, home, *habayt*…

Standing up, against all the usual 'forms' of things, standing up, even though Paul did lightly, faintly try to restrain her.

"*Toda raba / Merci beaucoup*…"

"No need to translate for me, I understand Hebrew as well as I understand my own name … *Toda raba* to you too, for having joined us tonight … and I hope you will join us permanently … forever and forever and forever … until you too are released from the satanic, evil flesh and become your real Self."

Bowing, head down, the way she used to bow during the Aleinu, when the Torah was taken out, as if the priest himself were some sort of latter day prophet, divine incarnation, as she sat down feeling all confused, as the women in the congregation began to go up to the altar in one line and the men in another, the women kissing the bible and the priest then holding the bible up to the man opposite her, the same place she had kissed it up against his lips, the men on one side, the women on the other, as the men came down kissing each other on both cheeks, the women kissing each other on both cheeks.

"What's going on?"

"The Kiss of Peace," explained Paul, "only the women can never touch the men or the men the women … the evil-flesh must not be tempted…"

Miriam thinking *What about homosexuality*? But not saying anything, getting in line with the women as Paul got in line with the men, when she got up to the front and kissed the bible, the priest smiling at her like some ancient Fiddler come down off the Roof to spread his inner joy to the world around him.

"So good to have you here."

"So good to be here."

Going back to her seat with the others, Paul back next to her, her tempted to tell him "*You'd better not sit next to me, it's a big sin*," but again said nothing, was ashamed, in fact, of her sarcastic, ridiculing mind that turned all of creation into one vast smirking joke. One final blessing.

"May Our Lord Jesus Christ descend upon us all and keep us away from the evil flesh, keep us oriented toward Him, toward the Holy Spirit that invisibly circles around us during our hopefully sinless days, as the Father sits upon His throne in Heaven and looks down upon us, waiting for us to join him forever. May we forever keep away from meat and eggs and milk, the flesh, never to sleep unclothed, always keeping our minds away from the flesh that we are temporarily clothed in until we move forever into fleshless beatitude … in omnia saecula saeculorum, Amennnnnnnnnnnn…"

Dragging out the "nnnnnnnnnn" for a full thirty seconds (she counted), bending down almost to the ground, his hat staying on his head with what Miriam laughingly thought of as miraculous stick-to-itiveness, then feeling ashamed again at seeing humorously what was, she felt on her deepest, deepest levels, a door into a Truth that once opened and stepped inside of, would give her a life, total … *simkha* … happiness … joy … beatitude…"

Then, once the priest had ended his "nnnnnnnnn," a sudden change taking place in everyone's mood, the whole atmosphere, a little woman with a short skirt, not in her first youth (surgery perhaps, old but not on the surface) giving her an embrace.

"I'm Maria … I almost said Marie Antoinette, but we're way behind that, aren't we?" ha, ha, ha, ha, a voice more like a cackling hen than anything human, "It's so nice to have you aboard … I was going to say 'the bus,' but maybe 'the ark' would be more appropriate," cackle, cackle, cackle, cackle…

A huge bull of a guy approaching from behind Maria, "*Je suis Louis Quatorze* / I'm Louis the Fourteenth," his laugh a double-bass version of hers, Miriam wondering *Do gorillas laugh? If they did that'd be* him *wouldn't it?* A gorilla or a bear. Or thunder. Then getting very serious, "I'm Louis, let's just leave it at that, it was a funny coincidence that a Louis should marry a Maria/Marie, but life is like that, *n'est ce pas?*"

"It certainly is. Who would have thought that I would have ended up here, of all places … among such…"

"Such a bunch of idiots, right?" a very bearded man behind her, looking like, what exactly, an orthodox Jew or Greek Catholic, shaving and barbering a sin, you had to leave yourself exactly the way God brought you into this world, reality is reality is reality and cannot not in any way be shaped or formed/deformed…

"On the contrary, it's a wonderful bunch here," Miriam feeling so very at home that it scared her. She wasn't at home, these weren't her people, but suddenly she *was* at home, and they were *hers, hers, hers* and she was *theirs, theirs, theirs…*

The priest approaching her, totally changed now, the medieval-prehistoric icon replaced by just a nice, bearded guy.

"Come on, Miriam," raising his voice, turning around, "all of you … it's snack and talk time, back to the 'castle,'" everyone beginning to leave the chapel, back into the mansion itself, all lit up now, the chandeliers all with little candle-shaped bulbs in them, all sorts of wall-lights, lamps, everything 'shaped' metal, curls and curlicues and fleur de lys, Miriam wondering how they managed to electrify such a place, the artist-architect in her imagining the work that must have gone on behind the walls to bring the whole place into the twentieth, twenty-first century, the priest, with his arm around her shoulder, lowering his voice, "So when can we begin 'classes?' I'm assuming you want to be one of us…"

"Any time," she said, feeling she was back in Tel Aviv and the priest was Rabbi Krongold, who had prepared her for her Bat Mitzvah and who she always put up on a pedestal as if he were little less than a representative/spokesman for The Divine.

"Let me give you a card. You can call me at your leisure … we're leisurely about things around here. After all, we have all eternity, *n'est ce pas?*"

Paul, behind her, smiling.

"I/we hope so."

As if they were married or something. He was her partner, spokesman, liking it and not liking it, not *really* wanting to get involved with anyone *that way*...

The priest reaching under his gown into his trouser pocket, pulling out a wallet and taking a little card out, handing it to her.

"Call me ... at your leisure ... at your leisure ... and now..."

Holding his arms out, hands up, like Bacchus, she thought without wanting to, toward a table in the main dining room spread out full of all sorts of little dessert-things that she was just beginning to learn the names of, *flans de marrons*, chestnut cream, surrounded by four little globs of yellowish/goldenish sorbet, apple tarts (*tartelettes)* full of pine nuts and yellow raisins, *nougats* full of honey and almonds, ashamed at herself for wondering how you could make *nougats* without eggs ... weren't eggs on the Verboten/Forbidden List?

"Not bad, huh?" said Paul.

"Excellent!"

Miriam just imagining herself bloating up and becoming a blimp, dirigible, a ripe persimmon (her favourite fruit, after mangos) ... everyone crowding around her.

A tall thin, grey-haired man with glasses, looking totally sexless, the kind of nerd who plays video games and watches sci fi movies all night long, coming over and touching her on the elbow.

"Nice elbows!"

"Franz!" Paul getting very defensive.

"Sorry! I'm an anatomist ... professor of anatomy ... haven't I seen you at concerts and things?"

"I go to what I can!"

Miriam trying to go to whatever concerts and plays and exhibits were around town in Toulouse, a lot going on really, although she still hadn't seen Debussy's *Pelléas and Melisande* on stage ... although she did have it on a DVD.

A big, roundish, globular blonde coming over to her, going into her purse and pulling out a fancy gold ballpoint that in spite of its ballpointedness still managed to look antique, Renaissance-ish...

"Let me give you my address and phone number. I'm Sarah Duchamp, a widow … I live just on the edge of town … excellent cook … not me but my cook…"

All sorts of thoughts swirling through Miriam's head, *I wonder, is your phone as Renaissance-looking as your ballpoint pen? What's all this food-madness, I thought the body was supposed to be evil, is the only thing evil about it sex?*

Looking at Sarah's gold, heel-less shoes, black tights, short gold dress with little gold balls sewn all around the bottom edge and around the edges of the short sleeves, wanting to ask her how she managed to not shiver and shake, Miriam herself, for all of her heavy sweater still chilly, although there was a huge fire in the huge fireplace at the end of the dining room, thinking that it really was like going back a few centuries…

"Sounds good," she said, feeling hypocritical.

Did she really belong here? Was this really primitive Christianity at its purest, or had Disneyworld taken over everywhere, suddenly thinking of the most sumptuously overdone department store in Paris, La Galerie Lafayette … being here almost like being there … the Renaissance updated and brought into modern times, noticing skirtingboard heaters all along the wall, all carefully painted white, with fleur de lyses in gold along their whole length … spring in the air today, but tonight mid-winterish again … suddenly wanting to be back on the beach in Tel Aviv, her inner voices speaking to the Arab world, *We're all the same thing, the same people, look at us, look, Salaam, Shalom* … remembering, when she was a kid, sometimes saying something to an Arab speaker and they'd think it was Arabic … *ma hadash … what's new…?*

"You're hardly here at all, are you?" Paul asking her as Sarah handed her a slip of paper with her name and numbers on it, Sarah blocking any answer with "Don't forget, when you're back in town, call me…"

"I will."

"Promise!"

"Promise."

And Sarah disappeared, so many other faces to face, sociability carried to obsessiveness, touching arms and kissing faces, *un, deux, un, deux* … if it wasn't on both cheeks it wasn't anything…

Walking over toward the fire with Paul beside her, an alternative self, feeling that, yes, she could totally, totally, totally trust him. Two big red chairs next to the fireplace, totally outside the Renaissance decor, Miriam, carrying her little seventeenth-centuryish-looking plate of sweets with her, sinking down into one of them thinking that the Renaissance wasn't very comfortable, was it, but these chairs were like half-materialized clouds, *parfait, parfait, parfait*. This strong impulse to just close her eyes and sleep. Sleep its own heaven, perchance to dream. Which was OK too, wasn't it, choose an island somewhere, like ancient, ancient Crete, Easter Island, and bring back dead husbands and sons and parents, aunts, uncles, the clan, blood, friends from school, former lovers … and never wake…

"It is a bit overwhelming, isn't it?"

"Buddhists are the same way," Paul sitting down next to her with his own little plate of goodies, relaxing too, but still sounding a bit defensive, "Once you have the body 'tamed,' then you're free to just *be*. Just look at the face of the Dalai Lama … like some ancient saint…"

"I'm feeling like an ancient saint myself," she smiled.

"Good. It's tempting to just close your eyes and 'rest' a while. We have a long ride back, after all…" smiling, "I wonder what's in these goodies?"

"Good things."

Finishing them up quickly, all sugary and spicy, full of fruits and delectability, not worrying about ingredients, recipes, just *there* all over her tongue, for an instant becoming pure gustatory-ness … then when they'd finished everything, putting the plates on a little table between the two chairs, next to a big picture book on Monet. Miriam feeling like putting the little table in front of her and sitting down and putting her legs up on it, but resisting the temptation, instead sinking down into the luxuriously cushioned chair, as Paul playfully whispered *"Un, deux, trois … sommeil … les yeux fermés, l'oreille aux rumeurs entrouverte, on ne dort qu'à demi d'un sommeil transparent…* / one, two, three … sleep … eyes closed, ears half open to sounds, you half-sleep a transparent sleep…"

Not really wanting to ask, but the book-worm in her still there, curious.

"Is that all you or…?

"Victor Hugo. 'June Nights.'"

End of March, but…

"Almost there…"

Closing her eyes, knowing that lots of the old ladies and old men would still have loved to bustle around and talk to her, but suddenly the whole party in the far distance, like she was scuba-diving off of Bermuda and the crackling sounds of the fire were bubbles and waves … a gentile, polite bunch … leaving her/them … totally alone … as she sank into a timeless moment of pure everythingness-nothingness…

X

She was a total Cathar now, every Friday night out to *Le Palais*, The Palace, as everyone called it, all sorts of new friends in Toulouse, part of a wealthy, aristocratic in-group society all of a sudden, always thinking that *no, the poor didn't want to be Cathars, they wanted the Here and Now, whatever they could eke out of the flesh, the spirit be damned…*

And, after long, long conversion-sessions with Father Lafayette (which she always thought was an ironic name for him, seeing that the biggest department store in Paris was also named Lafayette, but never asking if that's how he'd got his money), she was totally inside now, inside, inside, inside, convinced that this life was totally transient, that we had been so carefully created just to hardly touch ground, and then pass into heavenly foreverness, that the demons were for the most part in charge of this world, that the flesh was evil, contaminated, diseased, cancered and tumoured, always failing, fading, that from the minute we were born, if we were lucky enough to *be* born, beginning to fail, fade … convinced that all 'history' was was a record of the madness of man trying to hold on to this world, this little piece of land, this castle, this river, creating *Übermenschen*-supermen like the Germans had done, a whole philosophy of supermen who could crush everyone else, holocaust the Jews out of existence, or like the Catholics during inquisitorial times burning the 'heretics' at Montségur and every place else, whenever they could get their hands on them. And then the Muslim fanatics and jihad doing the same thing, everyone had to be Muslim or nothing. Either "Join my club, believe what I believe, or you're dead!" One wave of fanaticism after another, that was the whole of history, wasn't it? The Spanish in the New World destroying the Aztecs and Mayas, the Cross becoming a battering ram to batter down anything that disagreed with IT … *in the beginning was the Word and the Word was God and either you agreed with MY Word or you were fly-and-maggot-food …* what sense did birth defects make, or being born blind, retarded? What sense did earthquakes make, or volcanos, or asteroids like the one that had carved out the Pacific Ocean in ancient, ancient times?

As if there were anything but Evil in charge of this world. If Good was out there in charge, her husband wouldn't have been killed, nor her children, would they?

What sense did any of it make except as a prelude to Heaven, so that everything Here and Now was senseless, no God in charge of anything, but Chaos Demons in charge of it all … as we stepped out of the flesh into Eternity.

All the Catharist friends she made had made her life so much more agreeable, dinners here and there, concerts, plays, all the old (sexless, beyond sex) guys and gals, hardly anyone young in the group, so that it looked like when they died the whole thing would die out with them. Only, after she'd said that one night to a new friend, Gladys Couroux, a sculptress who made tiny little sculptures out of semi-precious metals and semi-precious stones, very much like Camille Claudel's sculptures she'd seen in the Rodin museum in Paris when she was still living there … when she'd told Gladys "How do you expect the Cathars to survive after the present group is gone?"

"I won't have to worry about it, will I? Although, when the media-obsessed 'youngsters' get old, then maybe they'll turn to Truth, when all the screens and control panels are meaningless to them. I'm not much for proselytizing, are you?"

"Not really. I just *happened* to find you…"

"And they'll just *happen* to find us, even after we're gone. We never really did die out, did we, no matter how many of us they burned to death!"

Something inside her wanting so much, so much, so much to be close to Montségur, as if the spirits of the martyrs were still there waiting for her, getting up one Wednesday morning feeling she *had* to go down there, *be* there for a while, calling up Paul.

Five rings before he answered.

"Hello."

"It's me, Paul. I'm going to Montségur. Just for a visit. If I'm not at services on Friday night, tell Father Lafayette, OK? You wouldn't want to come with me…?"

Thinking for a moment.

"I'd like to, of course, but … I don't want to say the word 'old,' but…"

Old he was, and older he would be.

"Understood. OK, my friend, blessings … *je t'aime…*

"*Moi aussi,*" uncertainly mumbled, and then, as if the uncertainty wasn't enough, "In my own way."

"In my own way too," she laughed, hung up, wondering, a little bit guiltily, if he ever did or had had anything sexual at all, or was he always up in the clouds, on the top step of the stairway to heaven? Which was the impression he gave, that he was totally divorced from the flesh and fleshly cares, except for his lung problems and arthritis problems and problems with sleeping, which he semi-solved with herbs, herbs, herbs…

Put a few things in a bag, underwear and tights, a couple of skirts and tops, sweaters, soaps and toothbrush and all her toiletries in a little leather bag her dead husband had given her on a Chanukah that seemed like centuries earlier.

Stopped for petrol on the way, got a map and sat there and marked it with a red marker she had in the glove compartment for just that purpose.

Spring everywhere around her, and the further she got out of town and into the sprawling, mountainous landscape, the more ebullient, ecstatic, beatific she felt, as if the Beatific Vision wasn't in the Great Beyond somewhere but in this very intense, condensed, delicious Now.

The voices inside her always talking, though, debating everything she thought/felt, *it's so beautiful, isn't it, the peasants out there in their fields, how many cancers, how many dead infants at childbirth, how much AIDS, how many alcoholics, how much arthritis and how many bent, torturous backs, how many retardees and crazies … remember the countries where forty percent of the population has AIDS, remember Vesuvius and The Great Flood … and what about beauty contests in Nigeria…? How many murders in New York, Detroit, Los Angeles last year?*

And that's what she *really, really, really* believed, wasn't it? That under the surface of whatever may appear good, it was basically, essentially evil, the demons *were* in control of the world, her imagination suddenly filled with images out of Hinduism and Chinese art, the gargoyles atop Notre Dame, if you were going to pray you'd be better off praying to demons rather than the gods/God … ADONAI ECHAD/One God … something she couldn't shake out of her head, that had been etched in her spirit as a girl … one God, one, one, one, one…

Opening all the windows in the car, letting the wind do what it wanted with her hair, sometimes the smell of cow-shit or horse-shit coming in across her for a moment as she'd pass a farm, smiling as she actually enjoyed the smell that whispered its own message, *it's coming back, the yearly resurrection*, all the trees and bushes alive with new leaves, loving the winter landscape, saying to herself lots of times that she *preferred* it, but not really, loving the idea of being enveloped in leafdom, sometimes when she'd pass a farmhouse on a hill somewhere, the ploughed, sprouting fields next to it and always in the distance forest, forest, forest, something inside her saying *This is where you belong, your ancestral cro-magnon, neanderthal you, the you that saw the forest as home, the same way that squirrels and deer, racoons, badgers … and monkeys, hyenas, great apes, do…* something in her just wanting to stop and merge with the forest, sometimes wondering how there could be so much forest left after all the thousands of years that southern France had been inhabited…

Crying sometimes when her boys would start screaming at her in the wind, *bring us, back, mummy, there must be a way for you to bring us back, give us a chance to grow up, be men, have jobs, wives, our own children, remember how grandpa used to always talk about carrying on the name, shem, shem, shem*, then hearing the word 'shame', fragments of ancient services rattling around in her mind, *shem kevod malcuto*, hearing long-dead Cantors from her long-dead past singing ancient melodies that must not have been too different from what you would have heard if you'd gone into a temple in ancient Sumeria thousands and thousands and thousands of years ago…

Crazy, feeling crazy, getting to Montségur in early evening, amazed at how accurate her driving had been, laughing to herself, "I should have been a truck driver!"

Instead of what…?

She'd practically stopped drawing and painting, hadn't she. Maybe it was time to revive all that, become Monet-ish again, return to Impressionism, which she more and more saw not as a painting movement at all, but some sort of religious cult that said "God is everywhere!"

Slapping herself in the face!

"There you go again, *akshanit,* stubborn!"

Inviting the demons in to surround her, bring her back to Reality … this one little farmhouse just off the road, with a perfect view of Montségur itself. Pulling into the driveway, not herself any more, but some other alternative her taking over, in charge, at first not even sure it *was* Montségur there behind the house, a huge moon starting to rise over the horizon, taking up the whole sky, wondering why the moon on the horizon was always so large, the harvest moon, and then by the time it got to the apex of the heavens, becoming small, a small little ball, after it had been such a huge smirking face…

Was that Montségur or not?

Getting out of the car, still not herself, going to the door and knocking, first a little tap, then louder…

The knock of Destiny, the knock of God, the Demons, the knock of The Inquisition looking for more heretics to burn, suddenly her mind filled with the image of the 500 Cathars, like herself, who had been burned at the top of Montségur in the thirteenth century, talk about Muslim fanaticism, what about the Holy Roman Apostolic Church in the old days? Believe or else!

A skinny old man opening the door, his skinny old wife just behind him, scared, disturbed. Obviously no one ever knocked on their old, half-rotten, much-needing-paint door.

"*Oui?*"

"Is that Montségur in the background or not?"

"Who are you? No tourists around here. This is a private home. My wife is very sick."

"Sick with what?"

Starting to close the door on her. Which totally angered Miriam.

"No one closes the door on God!"

"God?"

Opening up again. Curious.

"Or demons!" Starting to close it again. Miriam pushing back, convinced that with just a little more pushing the door would come down altogether. "Are you crazy? I'm just a tourist looking for a room for a few days. And I'll pay well…"

A look passing between the old farmer and his wife, the wife wordlessly nodding a humble little YES, and the door opened up.

"We don't usually … but there is an extra room … you're Parisian…?"

"Originally from Tel Aviv, the Mound of Spring, I live in Toulouse now."

Le Tertre du Printemps…? / Tel Aviv. No hint. Did they even have television? Looking around the living room as she walked in. Nothing there. There was a lamp in the corner, electricity, though. "Toulouse … busy place … let me show you the room."

Following the old man into a side bedroom that … incredible / *incroyable,* faced right on Montségur.

"How much?"

"*Plus tard / Later…*"

The old guy would have to talk it over with his wife.

Miriam going out and getting her bag, coming back in as the old man explained that things weren't very modern, there was an out-house out behind the house, a cistern for the water, but it hadn't rained much this year, it was always a problem, water, there were springs but they were so far away, "That's what you get for living in the mountains … but it's great for grapes here … grapes and flowers…"

The old lady coming over and shaking hands.

"*Je suis Antoinette* … our families have lived here for … centuries … centuries…"

"We could have moved to the city, I know so much about wines … but … I'm Jacques…"

"And I'm Miriam."

"Beautiful name," said Antoinette, "so…"

"Biblical?"

"That's it! Biblical!"

Miriam feeling that she'd just walked out of the bible

herself, as Antoinette led her into her little room, wondering how they could be so trusting, a stranger out of the dusk coming into their house, and everything OK, as if terrorism didn't exist, it was the 'old days', some primitive, ancient time when Goodness oozed out of the sky and we were all brothers (and sisters) of the same vast family ... as if such a time had ever existed ... Fiddler on the Roofish ... in old Jewish colonies after the diaspora, maybe ... Lithuania, Russia, Bohemia, Germany...

"You've eaten?" asked Antoinette.

"Not really, but I have some, you know, nutrition-bars, with me; a couple of them and a can of juice will do it for me. I always travel prepared."

Always with a kind of emergency kit in her travelling bag, as if she expected the Nazis to knock on the door at any time and she'd have to climb up on a roof or hide in a basement until the demons had disappeared.

Sitting down on the bed.

"I'd be happy to warm you up some food. I always have left-overs. I always overcook ... I should get a smaller frying pan, I always have to fill up the one I have, and then we can never finish it up..."

"No, that's OK, I'm fine, really..."

Miriam feeling a little guilty for having pigged up on chocolate bars that afternoon when she'd stopped for petrol, not *really* hungry at all. Mainly tired.

Not wanting to even shower or wash her hair or anything else. She hadn't slept too well the night before, with this trip in the back of her mind, not fully articulated but still there...

"OK, I'll just leave you alone then, we stay up a little longer, until it's pitch black – except for the moon, which seems like a searchlight tonight, *n'est ce pas*? We'll be as quiet as two mice ... not that mice are that quiet..."

Laughing as she backed out of the door, something almost balletic about her movement, as if she were moving to the heard-only-to-her sounds of some magic guitar. A cute old woman, Miriam wishing she would be something like that, a vigorous, but at the same time delicate 'peasant' look, no huge cloud of Melancholia constantly shedding its rain down on her, but totally inside of the Now, as long as she had a Now to be inside of. After Antoinette had left, Jacques coming in, all smiles, "So sleep well..." having to add (the bones and brass side of the family) "We can talk about prices tomorrow ... for years I've been thinking about creating a little tourist something-or-other out of part of my land, we seem to be getting more and more 'famous' around here. Not that terrible things didn't happen in the past, but now ... there is something very special about around here, that's why the castles were built up on the hills in the first place..."

Obviously having a lot more to say, but he didn't say it, restrained himself, gave her a break.

"And the toilet?"

Motioning for her to follow him, a little 'hut' in back.

A big, newish flashlight in his hand as he came back into the house.

"It's not the *Côte D'Azur*, but it's home."

Just a little trite, but...

"Goodnight."

"Sleep well," handing her his flashlight, "Keep this, I have another one. Although you won't be needing any flashlight tonight. Not with this moon..."

Looking up at the moon, the fullest she had ever seen it, turning the landscape around them into a glorious study in rolling hills, shadows and summits, loving this part of France, Paris and around Paris so boringly flat when you came right down to it, thinking of herself as a hill-girl, a mountain goat, smiling, coming inside for a moment, then, as he went into the bedroom on the other side of the kitchen from hers with one last "*Bon Nuit*," going out again, not even using the flashlight until she got inside the out-house, toilet paper, yes, on a little roller next to the wooden toilet seat ... quaint ... everything 'quaint,' even the smell 'quaint.'

It was like going to a kibbutz somewhere out in the almost-desert. Or even more primitive than that, a trip back in time to the time when the lords of southern France ruled, and Versailles was still a dream to be dreamed. What if the southern lords had found a king among them and the capital of France had been down here instead of circum-Paris? What a different country it would have been, more Mediterranean, more 'Hebrew', semitic, more colourful, more a continuation of the ancient Sumerian, Egyptian, Phoenician past instead of being so 'mental' and 'northern...'

And she *could* almost get along without a flashlight, her and her almost-cat eyes, amazing, as she got older instead of getting blinder, it seemed that the acuity of her night-vision was growing, that she was turning into a bat, cat, owl...

Back into the house, the sound of a TV in their room. Wondering, could they have a dish somewhere, or were they just picking up whatever they could from Toulouse and the other towns around, something she'd ask about tomorrow.

Now she was so, so tired, trying to remember the names of the other towns around here, Carcassonne ... wasn't that one of them ... knew them, but her brain wasn't working...

One last little strawberry-flavoured nutri-bar, taking her herbs as usual, one capsule of Hops, another of Passion Flower, another of Skullcap. Not that she needed them. Nor needed the earplugs that she put in her ears. Nonsense, but ... *les rossignols, les rossignols, les rossignols*, the nightingales, nightingales, nightingales...

Smiling.

What nightingales?

Imagining David was with her as she climbed into bed, there to wrap around the way she used to sleep with him, one spirit, one flesh, all night long.

A melatonin (1 mg), peppermint-flavoured, under her tongue.

Off, off to dreams.

Baruch ata Adonai ... Holy are Thou, God...

David coming toward her. Where were they? Was heaven really just all one vast cloud-beach, moving toward him

"*It's been so long.*"

"*Like centuries.*"

"*But we finally made it... don't you miss the street-vendors?*"

"*Not really, now that I have you again...*" and they blurred together into one single being, Montségur and history, outhouses and inhouses, TV dishes and TVs, computers and terrorists all gone, gone, gone as she experienced the greatest orgasm she'd ever had in her life, spontaneously divine, divinely spontaneous, but still not emerging from dream, separating from him for a moment as they walked the cloud-dunes toward the distant cloud-sea, knowing that it would only be a matter of moments, minutes, before they spliced together again, *olam, haolam* /forever, the universe … again…

Awakened by the sunlight.

Dawn.

The sun hardly up yet.

Rising over Montségur.

Giant cumulus clouds, but the sun was like some ancient warrior cutting them into bits, shining forth in all its splendour, clouds and castles and the giant hill-peak itself…

It was Psalm 148 … coming into her mind in Hebrew, her favourite Psalm …

HALLELUJAH, HALLELUJAH, ET-ADONAI MIN HASHAMIM, HALLELUHU BAMROMIM, HALLELUHU, CAL MALAKHAV…

PRAISE YE THE LORD, PRAISE YE THE LORD FROM THE HEAVENS, PRAISE HIM IN THE HEIGHTS, PRAISE YE HIM ALL HIS ANGELS, PRAISE YE HIM, ALL HIS HOSTS, PRAISE YE HIM, SUN AND MOON, PRAISE HIM, ALL YE STARS OF LIGHT…

PRAISE THE LORD FROM THE EARTH, YE DRAGONS AND ALL DEEPS, FIRE AND HAIL, SNOW AND MIST, STORMY WIND FULFILLING HIS WORD, MOUNTAINS AND HILLS, FRUITFUL TREES AND ALL CEDARS, BEASTS AND ALL CATTLE, CREEPING THINGS AND FLYING FOWL, KINGS OF THE EARTH AND ALL PEOPLE, PRINCES AND ALL JUDGES OF THE EARTH…

PRAISE YE THE LORD…

And suddenly the demons weren't there any more, no demons in charge of anything, anything at all, all of it invented, all the crap and bullshit, all there was was Him, Him, Him, above us all, inside of all of us, inside of all of it, the whole universe Him, Him, Him…

And suddenly she was a primal, primitive, essential, stripped-of-all nonsense and modernity,

Jew

again.